APOLLINAIRE | The Amorous Adventures of Prince Mony Vibescu Les Onze Mille Verges

7123297

Ben

1971

HERTFORDSHIRE LIBRARY SERVICE

This book is due for return on or before the date shown. You may extend its loan by bringing the book to the library or, once only, by post or telephone, quoting the date of return, the letter and number on the date card, if applicable, and the information at the top of this label.

RENEWAL INFORM- ATION

The loan of books in demand cannot be extended.

L.32A

COUNTY
RESERVE STOCK

RETURN TO
COUNTY LIBRARY BOOKSTORE
TAMWORTH ROAD
HERTFORD   RTS. SG13 7DG
TEL. 56863 TELEX 81512

RETURN TO
HODDESDON
DESDON 62296

LOAN

10 JUL 1976
CANNOT BE RENEWED

7 AUG 1976

5 MAR 1977
30 APR 1977
30 APR 1977

7 OCT 1989

CANNOT BE RENEWED

6 SEP 1976

-2 SEP 1989

28 OCT 1989

JAN 1977

16 DEC 1989

D1321318

Les onze mille verges

GUILLAUME APOLLINAIRE

Les
onze mille verges

or

*The Amorous Adventures of
Prince Mony Vibescu*

*Translated from the French by
Nina Rootes
and with an Introduction by
Richard N. Coe*

PETER OWEN · LONDON

ISBN 0 7206 0174 6

All Rights Reserved. No part of this publication
may be reproduced in any form or by any means without
the prior permission of the publishers.

Translated from the French
Les onze mille verges
ou *les amours d'un Hospodar*

HERTFORDSHIRE
COUNTY LIBRARY
F.
H\1976
7123297

PETER OWEN LIMITED
20 Holland Park Avenue London W11 3QU

First British Commonwealth edition 1976
© 1973 Société nouvelle des Éditions Jean-Jacques Pauvert
English translation © 1976 Peter Owen Ltd.

Printed in Great Britain by
Villiers Publications Ltd London NW5

Les onze mille verges

In the title of this work Apollinaire is making an untranslatable pun. A *verge* means both a rod or a switch and, anatomically, a penis. A *vierge* is a virgin. During the fifth century, eleven thousand (*onze mille*) virgins, followers of St. Ursula, were massacred by the Huns in Cologne.

Portrait of Apollinaire. Drawing by Irène Lagut.

Introduction

Guillaume Apollinaire (1880-1918) was a poet, one of the most original France has given to the world. He was not a novelist – even when he wrote novels, his only delight was to fill them with poetry. And yet, for most of his working life, ill-paid for the dreariest of hack-work – as a clerk in a characteristically unsuccessful bank, as the all-too-bored sub-editor of an optimistic financial gazette for the small investor – he was under constant pressure to write novels for the most banal and the most basic of reasons: money. In the year 1907, as now, novels sold better than poetry, particularly poetry which was half a century ahead of its time. At the age of twenty-seven, more pressed than ever for cash and richer than ever with new ideas, he allowed himself to be tempted by the offer of a small printer-publisher in Malakoff, a suburb on the southern outskirts of Paris, to try his hand at catering for what was then known as the 'clandestine' market. In the event, neither of the two collaborators made his fortune, still less his reputation. But the outcome was two quickly-composed, short erotic novels, the first of which was *Les Mémoires d'un jeune don Juan*, while the second was *Les onze mille verges*. Their existence has puzzled, provoked and exasperated the critics ever since.

Poets of genius – particularly poets inspired with the kind of enchanting and sophisticated *naïveté* which characterizes Apollinaire – are not commonly expected to write pornography. Partly for obvious moral reasons, partly also because the purely erotic novel belongs to a genre in which it is so difficult to succeed that few serious authors care to risk their literary reputations among its many pitfalls. In some ways similar to the detective story, the erotic novel can only succeed as true literature by transcending itself, by using its stereotypes and its conventions to explore unex-

7

pected levels of awareness, whose significance in turn reflects back
on and endows with new meaning the simple acts of sexuality.
But these acts in themselves are so monotonous and so repetitive
that those writers who have genuinely succeeded in exploiting this
intransigent raw material may count as the rarest among the
rare. There was the Marquis de Sade, who used the form to shed
light on the secret and forbidden depths of human motivation
and to reveal the deadly flaws in the sentimental rationalism of
his times. There was Georges Bataille, the anthropologist, who
employed it to suggest the unsuspected links between religious
mysticism and orgiastic ecstasy. There was, and still is, Jean
Genet, whose own almost indescribable experience of sexual deg-
radation flowers into a vision of the haunting poetry of a universe
filled with symbols. More marginally, perhaps, there was Rabelais,
for whom the whole miracle of man was a new-discovered source
of wonderment, the sordid no less than the sublime; or D. H.
Lawrence, a man resolved to teach those puritanical hypocrites,
the Anglo-Saxons, that sex was not just something nasty that
happened in the woodshed, but a brave and a beautiful experience to be lived out unashamedly in the brilliance of spring sun-
shine. But the failures – those who titillatingly nauseate or
spuriously reveal, those who masturbate in the throes of imaginary
acrobatics, or fling down the gauntlet to the whole of Western
civilization with the vocabulary of a juvenile delinquent . . . the
failures are legion. And it is tempting at first sight, for all his
genius, to class Apollinaire among them.

Over and above the monotony of the subject matter, which
with each succeeding episode implacably compels the writer to
delve deeper and ever deeper into the abnormal, the improbable
and the uncomfortable in order to sustain at least a flicker of
interest, there are other, even more intractable difficulties to be
overcome. First and foremost, there is what might be called, in
Roland Barthes' term, an 'extreme disparity of structure' between
the original experience and the resultant literature – a disparity
perhaps greater than in any other genre. If – to illustrate the
Structuralist thesis – a writer is involved in a car crash; and if

later he describes the experience of that car crash in a novel, then he is not simply transposing a constant from one medium to another, but rather creating a wholly *new* structure in a completely different medium. The structure of the original experience was and remains complete in itself : physical, three-dimensional, clearly situated in space and time. The new structure is similarly complete and autonomous. Abstract, linguistic and imaginary, it is governed wholly by the laws of grammar and logic, as opposed to the laws of gravity and momentum which ordered the structure of the lived experience. Between the two 'structures' there is no direct, certainly no obvious or ascertainable relationship; a writer's life is wholly irrelevant to any but the most superficial understanding of his writing; and if there *appears* to be a relationship of cause-and-effect between the one and the other, this is, in the last analysis, nothing but Illusion – precisely that Illusion which it is the aim of literature to create.

In the pornographic novel, however, the disparity between the various 'structures' involved is so great that the Illusion tends to break down of its own accord, without there being any need of a Barthes to send it toppling. The experience – intense, overwhelming, exalting, miraculous – of a sexual act successfully shared between lovers is grotesquely different from the experience of that same act as witnessed by the uncommitted observer, be he the scientist or Peeping Tom. The miracle 'restructures' itself in terms of grunts and contortions, the exaltation dislimns into the ludicrous. And when this *voyeur* – and every writer of pornography is by definition a *voyeur*, at least in his own imagination – transmutes his observed experience into a structure of words, and when the words themselves are transmuted into yet another structure, which is that of the reader's mind and of the emotions consequent upon his imaginings, then progressively the gap gets wider and wider, and the structures less and less capable of sustaining the illusion of a truth. Falsity, rather than fantasy, is the hall-mark of the genre.

The pornographic poet, moreover, is faced with a difficulty which no writer in any other field has to reckon with, at least to such a degree. There is absolutely no way of calculating the emotional effect on the reader of almost any significant word he uses. He may nauseate, he may anger; he may exalt, he may arouse; he may conjure up giggles, or sniggers, or yawns, or dreams; his reader may ring for the police, or write to *The Times,* molest a teenager or make love to his wife. In the old days of clandestinity and secret sales under disreputable counters, there was at least a reasonable chance that he might at least excite, perhaps provoke – but even that suggestion of a certainty has now vanished. The words – poor, stunted, miserable, four-letter things that they are – go forth from him, to settle at the whim of chance on any one among a million unpredictable variants of Mind. And what new 'structure' they may produce there, God alone knows. Certainly the author doesn't.

The pattern of the pornographer's world, then, is that of a Dream, a Dream peopled with glossy plastic marionettes whose penises erect jerkily into action at the twitch of a G-string. And to this world, incontestably, belong all the stereotypes of *Les onze mille verges:* Mony the Hospodar, rich, vaguely exotic, even more vaguely aristocratic, furnished above all with the wealth, the refinement and the leisure which alone make indulgence in exquisite eroticism a conceivable possibility; Cornabœux, massive, brutal and proletarian, offering that indiscriminate promise of virility which the Dream invariably attributes to the manual worker, to counterbalance the sexual subtleties of his employer and master; and of course, all the women with the exception of Kilyemu, and of that strange figure, the politically-minded Polish nurse, whose stomach, used as a drum, alerts the Japanese and thus ensures the ultimate defeat of Tsarist Russia in the historical Battle of Mukden . . . and of whom more later.

In the Dream, there are no problems and no complications : no feminine frigidity or masculine premature ejaculations. Every man and every woman is immediately available upon demand, and multiple orgasms are the order of the day no less than of the night. In luxurious boudoirs decorated with obscene Japanese prints, but no more frequently than in cafés devastated by bombardment, orgasms succeed each other with the rapidity of rounds from an automatic rifle. Alexine, in the course of her second bout with Cornabœux, comes fourteen times in about as many seconds, while the duller, merely proletarian Cornabœux manages no more than three. Groups form, coalesce, de-coalesce only to reform immediately; quintets succeed trios, and full orchestras octets. Homosexuality alternates with lesbianism, masturbation with bestiality; vampires succeed transvestites and antiquated crones ravishing Lolitas. But one and all, in this Utopia, are equally and splendidly potent; and in the end, if not always at the beginning, all are equally willing. The Dream can be all things to all people : a strip-cartoon illustration to Havelock Ellis, a sex-maniac's vade-mecum, a psychoanalyst's field-day, a literary critic's peep-hole into the sweet sadisms and succulent masochisms of his pet poet, a moralist's text-book for a sermon on Hellfire . . . and the plain man's (or woman's) invitation to an inferiority complex. *So* rigid, *so* willing, *so* often . . . and they *never* get tired.

Inasmuch as he abides by the conventions of the Dream, Apollinaire is no more than what he sets out to be : a literary hack. But beside the hack, there are in Apollinaire three other, and greater, men : the Pole (his real name was Kostrowitzky) who for all his Frenchness, was irremediably involved in the misfortunes of his country and indeed in the politics of all the Slavic people; the pessimist, haunted by a vision of evil, of autumn waiting to transform the beauty of spring into a dirty pile of decaying leaves, and death always at the end :

> *Les feuilles*
> *Qu'on foule*
> *Un train*
> *Qui roule*
> *Le vie*
> *S'écoule. . . .*

and the poet, for whom words were the material of magic, and who could rarely write a dull or a repetitive phrase, even in the dullest and most repetitive of descriptions. It is the Pole who, every now and then, slides backwards out of the Dream, back with a bump into reality; it is the pessimist who gropes forward in anguish and transmutes the Dream, episode by episode, into nightmare; and it is the poet who signs the Dream so indelibly with his own name (even if it is only 'the abrupt pop of an *Apollinaris* cork') that it is hard to imagine that there can ever have been any serious doubt about his authorship. And there is also, dimly visible in the background, the shadow of yet a fourth figure behind the hack : Apollinaire the philosopher.

The obvious literary ancestor of most standard pornography is the Gothic Novel : the orgies and the flagellations take place in a nameless land of dark-walled mansions, or of deserted villas by the side of cold grey seas. Bluebeard's country has no known constitution, while Bluebeard himself reads no newspapers and we are unlikely ever to learn the rateable value of his castle. The country of the Dream is Utopia back-to-front, but still Utopia in its essential unreality, its anonymity : a faceless Cloud-Cuckoo-Land, *not* accessible by Green Line bus.

By contrast, the real world intrudes constantly into *Les onze mille verges,* sometimes in quite small ways, in street names or behind easily-lifted masks,* but sometimes so imperiously as to dictate the whole structure of the novel. Set quite specifically in the years 1903-5, the faceless landscape of the Dream is suddenly shaken by the rude reverberations of Balkan politics. The Black

---

* The rue de Prony and the rue Duphot, for instance, are real streets still existing in Paris, the one near the Parc Monceau, the other near the Madeleine. The name of the actress 'Estelle Ronange' clearly hides the reality of Marguerite Moréno, notorious for her public quarrels with Jules Claretie, the Administrator-General of the *Comédie française.* 'Adolphe Terré' and 'Tristan de Vinaigre' constitute hardly impenetrable disguises for Adolphe Retté and Tancrède de Visan, two minor symbolist poets. And the popular journalist André Barre is not lost for ever under the pseudonym of 'André Bar'.

Mass orgy in Bucharest is on the face of it just one orgy among others – until the sudden intrusion of the names of Alexander Obrenović and of his 'whore of a wife', Draga Mašin. For this is no longer fiction, but fact. Or at least, partially fact. Apollinaire's procedure here is extremely interesting, and in a curious way reminiscent of the 'collage' technique which he developed in painting, in which imaginative drawing is made to harmonize with 'real' objects – old bus tickets, pieces of string, newspaper cuttings, and the like.

For, on 10 June, 1903, a political secret society known as the 'Black Hand' did in fact contrive the murder of the last of the Obrenović rulers of Serbia, King Alexander, of all his male relatives, and of his consort Queen Draga. The epithet 'whore of a wife' is – in this context – literally significant; for whereas on the one hand it is perfectly consonant with the standard string of obscenities which characterize the speech of every personage in the novel, it also happens to be historically accurate. Not content with exercising through his Minister, Dr Vladan Gjorgjević, a policy of reaction and oppression over his restless people, Alexander had added insult to injury by marrying, in the summer of 1900, the divorced wife of an army officer, a woman considerably older than himself, dynastically unacceptable because she was known to be incapable of bearing children, and morally repugnant as queen in view of her numerous and flagrant infidelities.

This unexpected intrusion of political vituperation into the pornographic novel, rare as it is in modern literature, was not wholly Apollinaire's invention. It had been practised to some effect at the time of the French Revolution, and notably by Nerciat in his *Julie Philosophe ou le bon patriote* (1792), a novel with which Apollinaire was undoubtedly familiar, and which he later edited in a series entitled *La Bibliothèque des Curieux* (1910). But what is entirely original in *Les onze mille verges* is the intermediate degree of 'realism' which Apollinaire carefully and disconcertingly introduces in the interstices between undoubted reality and unquestioned fiction. For no one would doubt that Mony, Culculine *et Cie* are inventions; and equally no one can query the fact that Alexander Obrenović and Draga Mašin had real existences and were really murdered. But what about Colonel Kolović and his wife Natasha? The names are probable, the political background is even more probable : the Black Hand existed most effectively, and most of its members were disgruntled officers such as Colonel Kolović. Did Apollinaire simply take the name out of his morning newspaper? Apparently not. No Kolović appears in the records of the period. So it seems that Apollinaire was here inventing again, but inventing in a fascinating borderline area where only minute historical research can succeed in disentangling fact from fantasy.*

And it is precisely the same disconcertingly hybrid blending of fact and fiction we encounter in the other 'political' sections of the novel. For if Apollinaire, as a Slav, was fascinated by the violence of political events in Serbia, it is specifically as a Pole that he makes his most emphatic excursions into politics. The sadistic nurse who tortures and murders the Russian wounded is not merely a prophetic prototype of a breed later to be produced by Nazi Germany; she is lucidly and consciously taking revenge on the Russians who, in the later decades of the nineteenth century, and particularly under the régime of General Gurko, Governor General of the Province of Poland from 1883 to 1894, had systematically attempted to stamp out the last remnants of Polish national spirit and of Polish national culture. Apollinaire never gives us her name, but she describes herself as 'the daughter of the revolutionary prince, Jan Morneski', arrested by Gurko and sent to die in a prison camp in Tobolsk. Again, why not? It sounds so inherently probable. Yet the records are silent, and no Morneski appears among the list of Gurko's victims. It is as though Apollinaire, poet and patriot, not content with inventing his own fantasies, were also determined to invent his own history – and to force even the historians to accept it as reality.

---

* I am deeply indebted to Mr J. E. O. Screen, Librarian of the School of Slavonic Studies, University of London, and to his colleagues, for the research which they have carried out at my request in an attempt to establish the reality or otherwise of Apollinaire's 'intermediate' characters.

But clearly it is not so much the poet as the patriot who deter-
mines that the whole second part of the novel shall be set in the
middle of the Russo-Japanese War, which ended, with the catas-
trophe of Tsushima and with the surrender of Port Arthur, in
what was probably the most humiliating defeat in Russian history. Here political reality intrudes with a vengeance. The war
incidents described are the battle of Liao-Yang (26 August-4
September, 1904), and the beginning of the fatal battle of Mukden, which opened on 25 January, 1905, when General Grippen-
berg attacked the Japanese positions south-west of the city and
– as in the story, although possibly not for the same reasons –
was beaten back. General Stoessel ('the *valiant* General Stoessel',
Apollinaire calls him, in spite of, or perhaps *because* of the fact
that after the fall of Port Arthur he was court-martialled by the
Russians for cowardice and condemned to death) had a real
existence; so did Commander-in-Chief Kuropatkin and Admiral
Alekseyev; and so incidentally did Alekseyev's appeal to Kuropatkin (conveyed by Mony in his balloon) to come speedily to
the relief of Port Arthur. But by this time we are beginning
to look deliberately for the 'intermediary' figure, and sure
enough, there he is: General Munin. The Staff Lists of the
Russian Army during the battle of Liao-Yang are available
and they include all commanders down to Brigade level. We can
note the names of Major-Generals Fomin, Mingin, Churin and
Gribunin, among others. But no Munin. The patterns of Apollinaire's imagination are now becoming very clear. And while it
might be unwise to suggest that *Les onze mille verges* should be
studied as a history of the disasters which sparked off the 1905
revolution in Russia, there is clearly enough of reality in the novel
to mark Apollinaire off pretty clearly from the main run of
dreamers in Cloud-Cuckoo-Land.

If this intrusion of reality constitutes a first disconcerting element
in the novel, a second element is introduced by the overall uncertainty of tone. 'Uncertainty' here need imply no necessary criti-

cism of Apollinaire – rather the contrary. For it is as though two of the other, greater men in him – the pessimist now, backed by the poet – were struggling to find ways and means of making something out of the hack pornographer. And the most memorable pages of *Les onze mille verges* are those in which they succeed, even though it may be at the expense of the general stylistic unity of the novel.

For the genre, almost by definition, excludes two qualities, both of which are inherent in Apollinaire: humour and emotion. Pornography proper takes itself desperately seriously: it is unsmiling and unmoved; 'tenderness' is the dirtiest word in its vocabulary. But Apollinaire spent all his life being in love with almost everything; and a novel based on the murder of Love could evoke in him only two reactions – a wry and ironical smile at himself for writing it, and a despairing plunge into the ultimate of Evil. For Evil is the only force strong enough to murder Love; and if Love is murdered, then Satan is the only God left to whom to pray.

In the outcome, these two attitudes alternate throughout the novel, which is a neat, stylistic sandwich. At the outset, it is the irony that predominates. Then, suddenly, with the coming of Kilyemu, Love intrudes – and the murder of Kilyemu* is the murder of Love, and the beginning of the reign of Evil. But at the end, the irony returns – this time on an historical rather than on an individual level – and with self-mocking ingenuity the poet works out the triple pun implicit in the title.

The irony – the nearest that Apollinaire allows himself to get to humour – in the two outside slices of the sandwich shows itself as an obsessive urge to prick the bubble. Repeatedly, a scene will build up to its expected and improbable erotic climax, only to be interrupted with a comment or a tail-piece in flamboyant or sordid contrast, which cocks a retrospective snook at the stony seriousness of all that has gone before and dissolves the indigestible erotic hunks in the pungent broth of their own inherent absurdity. It is the literary equivalent of *coïtus interruptus*. A

---

* 'Kilyemu' = '[*Celle*]*qui l'émut*' ('She who moved him').

climax is shattered by 'a crystalline fart'. A scene of flagellation
– and no eroticists take themselves and their art more ludicrously
seriously than the specialists of the leather and the whip – col-
lapses into absurdity when the cab-driver from whom, in the
emergency, a whip had been purchased, is arrested by the local
traffic police for being in charge of a horse-drawn vehicle without
proper means of control. More often than not, where scatology is
used, it serves a similar purpose – namely that of deflating the
inherent pomposity of the genre. The description of Toné's body
– a typically Apollinairian rhapsody, with its 'splendid melons
ripened by the light of the midnight sun', its Greek temples and
its blocks of unflawed Carrara marble – explodes suddenly and
splendidly into 'the thighs were warm and the buttocks were
cold, which is a sign of good health', an application of the popular platitude 'a cold nose means a healthy dog' which, by its
studied inappositeness, is little short of surrealistic. Nor is it to be
forgotten that it was Apollinaire who first coined the word
'surrealism'. The episode of the washer-up and the young kitchen-
hand contains precisely that mixture of the grotesque, the absurd
and the sadistic that the later Surrealists would have enjoyed in
the Grand Guignol; and the misfortunes of Mony, detected as a
usurper in a bed not his own because he has only two balls
instead of the three sported by the legitimate occupant, seem to
anticipate the three noses of Eugène Ionesco's scrumptiously
edible heroine in *Jacques.*

But it is the Kilyemu episode which constitutes the true centre
and significance of the novel. The gentle, naïve, eternally innocent Japanese prostitute emerges suddenly out of the night, her
incorruptible spirit shedding an intolerable radiance of truth on
the corruption which surrounds her; and then, as quietly, she
vanishes:

> The little Japanese girl, straight-backed and solemn, went away
> like a shadow, leaving Mony, with tears in his eyes, to reflect
> on the fragility of human passions.

The coming of Kilyemu *could* have made *Les onze mille verges* into a novel of redemption. But if Kilyemu has affinities with Sofya Semyonovna, Mony is no Raskol'nikov, and Apollinaire no Dostoyevsky. Whether or not Apollinaire believed in God (as with most modern poets, the question, in its traditional form, is almost meaningless), he clearly possessed an intimation of the reality and of the immanence of Evil; and with the second appearance of Kilyemu the victory of Evil begins. It is Mony himself who murders Kilyemu, and from that instant Death takes over. The ensuing series of sketches – the advanced student's practical encyclopedia of sadism, not for the squeamish – has a quality of horror wholly absent from the earlier part of the novel. The irony and the absurdity have disappeared; in their place there is a cold, concentration-camp ferocity which increases with each successive episode. *Les onze mille verges* has been compared to *Justine* or to *Les cent vingt journées*. But the comparison is false. The Divine Marquis, for all his cynicism, still lived in the century of Voltaire. A part of him still longed to believe in the Rights of Man and the Goodness of Nature. Not so Apollinaire. This is the twentieth century, not the eighteenth. If Mony murders Kilyemu, it is not in protest against a God who has failed, but because Kilyemu as a person, dead or alive, is equally meaningless. The only reality of man is the body, not the spirit; the penis, not the soul – and the penis knows no law but its own satisfaction. The Battle of Mukden was the biggest orgy of destruction in modern history before 1914 – and by situating his orgy of rape and murder under the gunfire of the Japanese, Apollinaire transforms the Dream into an apocalyptic vision of evil and destruction. This is a far cry from Ronsard's lament *Car l'amour et la Mort n'est qu'une mesme chose,* which basically is what Genet is saying, and perhaps Beckett. It is the prophecy of a kingdom of disbelief and darkness, of indifference and absolute nihilism. The eroticism of the body is not merely ludicrous, it is evil – the ultimate Evil. The victory of the penis is the victory of Satan. Like all the great pornographers, Apollinaire, by this roundabout route, rejoins the Puritans : the triumph of the body is the murder of the soul.

This transformation of the Dream into a preview of that unprecedented mixture of personal sadism and political violence which characterizes our own time was the work of Apollinaire the poet and Apollinaire the pessimist working out their own individual variations on the conventional material of the pornographer. Apollinaire the philosopher – never the most impressive of the many men composing this complex being – plays little part in the operation. Yet the fact remains that Apollinaire *does* have ideas – they emerge, for instance, in *Les mamelles de Tirésias,* whose original draft was probably written at about the same time as *Les onze mille verges.* And there are traces of them here. Paradoxical ideas, but again, in a strange way, prophetic. In the Edwardian period – in France, *la belle époque* – the movement for what is now known as 'Women's Lib' was already making itself felt as a serious socio-political force. Apollinaire was not so much worried as perplexed. If the traditional relationship between women and men were to break down, what would happen to society? Who would do which part of the business of making the world continue to work? Who would repopulate a continent decimated by wars? And what would happen to lovers and to Love – and consequently to poets? In *Les mamelles* he half-seriously amused himself by showing the roles of men and women reversed: men bearing the children and rocking the cradles, women providing the lawyers and the generals and the politicians. But *Les mamelles* ends happily, whereas *Les onze mille verges* does not. If the conventional sexual relationships between men and women contain, by however remote an implication, the potential for evil and destruction which they reveal in Mony, then perhaps the only solution is for such relationships to cease altogether. Which leads to one of the most curious passages in the whole book – the Cossack officer's apology for masturbation, on the grounds that men and women not only should move, but already *were* moving, so far apart that within a foreseeable future it would prove to be the only form of sexual satisfaction available. Another paradox; and yet again a curiously penetrating insight. For if, in 1907, women's communes were unthought of, and the social acceptance of homosexual or lesbian groups unthinkable, the long-term result of a movement aimed at eliminating the distinction between the sexes may well, half a century later, prove to be having exactly the opposite effect. Which is something well worth bearing in mind before we dismiss Apollinaire's philosophy as wholly negligible.

In the last analysis, however, the man who remains is Apollinaire the poet; and it is the poet rather than the philosopher, or even the pessimist, who, in *Les onze mille verges* redeems the enforced banalities of the pornographer. We see him at work not only in the glittering lucidity of the style, not only in the brilliant parodies of his own and other poets' characteristic utterances with which the work is studded, but above all in the verbal variations which he weaves about that dreariest of all subjects : the literal description of the sexual organs of the human body. His portraits of women seem to take their origin in the sixteenth-century *blason;* each is original, distinct and memorable – even to the description of the tuft or fleece or beard of hair, black, ash-blonde or silver-gold, between their legs. Perhaps only Brantôme can offer such richness; and the most moving of all is again that of Kilyemu : 'a little peak of coarse black hair, like the tip of an artist's brush when it is wet'. None but a very remarkable poet could have created, in so few words and in such a context, a Kilyemu.

Les onze mille verges is not a pleasant book to read – but then neither is *Justine,* nor *l'Oeuf,* nor *Histoire d'O,* nor *Notre-Dame des Fleurs.* It is the unsolved paradox of sexuality that the same act can be wholly miraculous and utterly repulsive, not only to different people, but even to the self-same individuals involved, and not only at different moments in time but simultaneously. The 'libertine' novel, to use an eighteenth-century term – *Le Chevalier de Faublas,* or *The Philanderer,* or *Portnoy's Complaint* – disguises this fundamental paradox, often with wit, always with humour, sometimes with semi-decency as well. The pornographic novel reveals it – and thus, in spite of the unreality of the Dream, the description of the Dream is the mirror-reflec-

tion of a reality. But a reality, however unwelcome and un-
pleasant, is a kind of Truth. And poets are concerned with Truth.
And Apollinaire is a poet : even in *Les onze mille verges.*

University of Warwick   RICHARD N. COE
September 1974

Note to the Reader

Certain passages in the later part of *Les onze mille verges* could be considered exceptionally violent. In order not to jeopardize the publication of the book as a whole, these have been omitted. Such passages are indicated by parentheses in the text. Where necessary, in order to sustain the narrative flow of the novel, the substance of these passages is indicated briefly in footnotes.

Chapter 1

Bucharest is a beautiful city. Orient and Occident seem to meet and intermingle there, for although you are still in Europe, from a purely geographical standpoint, you have only to observe certain of the local customs, and to glimpse the picturesque specimens of Turkish, Serbian and other Macedonian races who are to be seen on the streets, to realize that you are already in Asia. Nevertheless, it is a Latin country. The thoughts of the Roman soldiers who colonized this land must have turned constantly towards Rome, the then capital of the world and source of all civilized refinements. This Occidental nostalgia has been passed down to their descendants, for the Roumanians dream incessantly of a city where luxury is the natural element, and life full of joy. However, since Rome has been stripped of her splendour, and has ceded her crown as Queen of Cities to Paris, it is hardly surprising if, by an atavistic phenomenon, the thoughts of the Roumanians are forever turned towards Paris, which has so deservedly supplanted Rome as the hub of the universe.

In common with his compatriots, the handsome Prince Vibescu dreamed of Paris, City of Light, where all the women are beautiful and every one of them is willing to part her thighs. While still at college in Bucharest, he had only to imagine a Parisian woman – *the* typical Parisienne – to get an erection and be forced to toss himself off, which he did slowly and in a state of beatitude. Later, he had spurted his seed into the cunts and arses of numerous delectable Roumanian women, but he felt an overpowering desire to have a Parisienne.

23

Mony Vibescu came from a very wealthy family. His great-grandfather had been a Hospodar, a dignitary position corresponding to a Sub-Prefect in France. The title was hereditary and both Mony's father and grandfather had called themselves 'Hospodar'. In honour of his grandsire, Mony Vibescu should likewise have borne this title, but he had read enough French novels to know that Sub-Prefects are something of a joke: 'Look here,' he said to himself, 'isn't it absurd to call oneself Sub-Prefect simply because one's great-grandfather was one? It's utterly grotesque!' And so, to appear less grotesque, he had replaced the title of Hospodar-Sub-Prefect by that of Prince. 'Now there is a title worth having!' he exclaimed to himself, 'and one which can honourably be passed on through the hereditary line. Hospodar is a civic function, and while it is perfectly correct that a man who distinguishes himself in the civil service should be given this title, I prefer to ennoble myself. After all, I too am an ancestor. My children and my grandchildren will have something to thank me for.'

Prince Vibescu was on intimate terms with the Serbian Vice-Consul, Bandi Fornoski, who, according to rumour, delighted in buggering the charming young Mony. One morning, the prince dressed in formal attire and set out for the Serbian Vice-Consulate. As he walked through the streets, all heads turned and the women ogled him saying: 'Isn't he just like a Parisian?'

And in fact Prince Vibescu copied the gait of a Parisian, that is to say, the gait which everyone in Bucharest imagines to be Parisian: with tiny, scurrying footsteps and waggling his bottom. The effect is charming! And when a man walks like that in Bucharest, there is not a woman who can resist him, no matter if she is married to the Prime Minister.

On arriving at the Serbian Vice-Consulate, Mony pissed profusely against the front of the house, then rang the bell. An Albanian dressed in a white *fustanella* opened the door. Prince Vibescu climbed rapidly to the first floor. Vice-Consul Bandi Fornoski was in his drawing-room, stark naked. He lay on a velvety sofa with his prick rampant. Beside him was Mira, a brunette from Monte-negro, who was tickling his balls. She too was nude and, as she was leaning forward, her fine, well-rounded arse, brown and downy, stuck out prominently, with the deli-cate skin stretched as tight as a drum. Between the but-tocks ran the deep and dark-haired furrow with the for-bidden hole showing as round as a cough drop. Beneath them stretched two long and lissom thighs and, since her position forced Mira to part them, Mony could see her cunt, thick, fleshy, deeply-cloven, in the shadow of a dense jet-black mane. She was not at all put out by his arrival. On a chaise-longue in another corner, two pretty girls with full round bottoms were poking their fingers up each other's arses and letting out little 'Ah's!' of volup-tuousness. Mony quickly took off his clothes, then, with his fully erect prick waving in the air, he threw himself upon the two lesbians and endeavoured to separate them. But his hands slipped on their damp and glistening bodies as they wriggled and writhed like snakes. Mony, seeing that they were drooling with sensual delight, and enraged at being unable to share in it, slapped the nearest fat white backside with the flat of his hand. As this seemed to excite the owner of the bottom considerably, he began to strike with all his strength, to such effect that, pain overcoming pleasure, the pretty girl with the reddened arse stood up angrily and said:

'Pig! Prince of bum-boys! Go away, we don't want your great big cock. You can give that stick of barley-sugar to Mira. Leave us alone, we want to make love in our own way, don't we, Zulmé?'

'Yes, Toné!' replied the other young woman.

The prince brandished his enormous prick, crying:

'What, you stupid sluts, can't you think of anything better to do than stick your fingers up each other's arses?'

Seizing one of them, he tried to kiss her on the mouth. It was Toné, a lovely brunette whose snow-white body was delightfully marked with beauty spots in just the right places, showing off the whiteness of her skin. Her face was equally white and a beauty spot on the left cheek lent an added piquancy to the girl's charms. Her chest was graced with two superb breasts as hard as marble, veined with blue and surmounted by delicate pink strawberries, the right one prettily marked with a beauty spot which sat there like a fly, a most provocative little fly.

Mony Vibescu, as he seized her, had passed his hands under her plump arse, which was so white and full that it could have been a splendid melon ripened by the light of the midnight sun. Each of her faultless buttocks seemed to have been carved from a block of Carrara marble, and her thighs descended with the perfect roundness of the columns on a Greek temple. But what a difference! The thighs were warm and the buttocks were cold, which is a sign of good health. The spanking had made them a little rosy, so that the colour of raspberries mingled with the cream of her skin. The sight of them excited poor Vibescu to the limit of endurance. His mouth sucked each of Toné's firm titties in turn, then, planting his lips on her neck and shoulder, he left strawberry marks. His hands kept a firm grip on her large bottom, which felt like a hard and full-fleshed water-melon. Fondling these royal buttocks, he inserted his index finger into an arsehole of exquisite tightness. His great prick, swelling more and more, moved like a battering-ram against a delicious coral cunt surmounted by a shining black fleece. She shouted at him in Roumanian: 'No, you're not going to put it in!' and at the same time she wriggled her round and chubby thighs. The inflamed red head of Mony's prick had already touched the entrance to Toné's moist grotto.

The girl escaped again, but with the sudden movement she let out a fart, not a vulgar fart, but a fart of crystalline delicacy which made her burst into violent and hysterical laughter. Her resistance slackened, her thighs opened and Mony's huge battering-ram had already buried its head in the redoubt when Zulmé, Toné's lover and partner in sex-games, seized Mony's balls roughly and, squeezing them in her little hand, caused him such pain that the smoking cock withdrew hastily from its niche, to the great disappointment of Toné, who was already beginning to stir her large arse.

Zulmé was a blonde, with a thick mane of hair falling right down to her heels. She was shorter than Toné, but yielded nothing to her in slenderness and grace. There were dark rings under her black eyes. The moment she let go of the prince's balls, he hurled himself at her, saying: 'Very well then, you will pay for Toné!' Seizing a pretty little tit in his mouth, he began to suck the tip. Zulmé twisted and turned. To tease Mony, she made undulating movements with her belly, at the base of which danced a delicious, tightly-curled blonde beard. At the same time, she lifted up her prominent mound of Venus, which was cleft by a sweet little cunt. Between the lips of this pink pussy dangled a rather long clitoris, giving proof of her tribadism. The prince's cock strove in vain to penetrate this recess. At last he clenched her buttocks in his fists and was about to pierce her when Toné, furious at having been thwarted of the discharge from his superb prick, started to tickle the young man's heels with a peacock's feather. He began to laugh, twisting this way and that. Still the feather tormented him, as it moved up from the heels to the thighs, to the anus, to the cock, which swiftly lost its erection.

Enchanted with their sport, the two little fiends, Toné and Zulmé, laughed for a long time, then, red-faced and breathless, they began their games again, embracing and

licking one another in front of the baffled and crestfallen
prince. Their bottoms rose and fell in cadence, their hair
intertwined, their teeth clattered together, their firm,
palpitating breasts rubbed against each other like the
ruffling of satin. At last, writhing and moaning with
pleasure, they came at the same moment, while the
prince's cock began to raise its head again. Seeing that the
two girls were exhausted from their mutual goosing, he
turned towards Mira who was still toying with the Vice-
Consul's prick. Vibescu approached softly and, passing
his splendid tool between Mira's plump buttocks, he slid
it into the moist and half-open cunt of the lovely girl
who, as soon as she felt the head of the penis pierce her,
jerked her arse backwards so that the weapon penetrated
completely. She continued these abandoned movements
while the prince stroked her clitoris with one hand and
tickled her nipples with the other.

His piston-like movements in her tightly-clenched cunt
gave Mira intense pleasure, as she proved by letting out
little squeals of delight. Vibescu's belly struck against
Mira's arse and the coolness of her buttocks gave the
prince as much pleasure as the warmth of his belly gave
to the young girl. Soon their movements became quicker,
more staccato, the prince pressed hard against Mira who
was panting as she squeezed her thighs together. The
prince sank his teeth into her shoulder and held her
firmly. She shouted:

'Ah! that's good ... hold on ... harder ... harder ...
oh, oh, take all of me. Now, give me your spunk ... all of
it ... yes! Yes! ... yes!'

And in the mutual ecstasy of orgasm, they sank down
and remained for a moment oblivious of everything.
Toné and Zulmé, entwined in each other's arms on the
chaise-longue, looked at them and laughed. The Serbian
Vice-Consul had lit a slim cigarette filled with Oriental
tobacco. When Mony stood up again, he said to him:

'Now, my dear Prince, it is my turn. I was waiting for you, and although I allowed Mira to titillate my cock, I have reserved the full enjoyment for you. Come, light of my life, my dear little bugger, come, let me slip you a length.'

Vibescu looked at him for a moment, then, spitting on the cock proffered to him by the Vice-Consul, he uttered these words:

'I am sick and tired of being your bum-boy, the whole town is talking about it.'

But the Vice-Consul, with his prick rampant, had stood up and seized a revolver. He pointed the gun at Mony who tremblingly offered him his posterior, stammering:

'Bandi, my dear Bandi, you know I love you, bugger me, please bugger me.'

The smiling Bandi forced his weapon into the elastic hole hidden between the prince's buttocks. Once it was in, and with the three women watching him, he jerked about like a madman, blaspheming the while:

'God's b . . . s! I'm coming, squeeze your arse, my pretty little fag, squeeze hard, I'm coming. Squeeze your pretty buttocks.'

And with haggard eyes, his hands clenched on Mony's fragile shoulders, he reached his orgasm. Afterwards Mony washed, dressed again and left, saying he would return after dinner. But, on reaching home, he wrote this letter:

'My dear Bandi,

I am sick of being buggered by you, I am sick of the women of Bucharest, I am sick of spending my fortune here, when I could be spending it so much more happily in Paris. Within two hours I shall be gone. I hope to enjoy myself immensely. Bidding you a fond farewell,

> Mony, Prince Vibescu
> Hereditary Hospodar.

The prince sealed the letter and wrote another to his solicitor asking him to liquidate all his assets and forward the entire sum to Paris, as soon as he should receive Mony's address there.

Taking all the loose cash he possessed, some 50,000 francs, Mony made his way to the station. He posted the two letters and boarded the Orient Express for Paris.

Chapter 2

'Mademoiselle, the moment I laid eyes on you I fell madly in love. I felt my genitals rise up in salute to your sovereign beauty, and my blood run as hot as if I had just drunk a glass of hot rum.'

'Oh, come, come!'

'I lay my fortune and my heart at your feet. If we were in bed together, I would prove my passion for you twenty times in succession. May I be punished by the eleven thousand *vierges,* or even eleven thousand *verges,** if I tell a lie!'

'Pie in the sky!'

'No, my feelings are sincere. I do not speak to every woman in this manner. I am no Casanova.'

'Oh sir, you bowl me over!'

This conversation took place one sunny morning on the boulevard Malesherbes. It was May, the month when nature is reborn, and the Parisian sparrows were chirruping their love songs in the newly-verdant trees. The gallant Prince Mony Vibescu made this declaration of love to an attractive young girl, slender and elegantly dressed, who was walking towards the Madeleine. She moved so fast that he had difficulty in keeping up with her. Suddenly, she turned round and burst out laughing:

'Come on then, let's get to the point. I'm in a hurry. I'm going to see a girl friend on the rue Duphot, but if you are prepared to entertain two women with a passion

---

* There is an untranslatable pun here, on *vierge* (virgin) and *verge,* which means both a rod or switch and, anatomically, the penis. The eleven thousand virgins referred to are the followers of St Ursula; according to legend, they were all martyred by the Huns, in Cologne, during the fifth century, though the date given varies.

31

for luxury and love, and if, indeed, you are a real man
in terms of both fortune and sexual prowess, come with
me.'

Mony drew his handsome figure to its full height,
announcing:

'I am a Roumanian prince and a hereditary Hospodar.'

'And I am Culculine d'Ancône,' she said, 'I am nine-
teen years old and I have already drained the balls of ten
men who were masters in the art of love and emptied the
purses of fifteen millionaires.'

Chatting pleasantly on a number of whimsical and
titillating subjects, the prince and Culculine reached the
house on the rue Duphot. They took the lift to the first
floor.

'Prince Mony Vibescu . . . my friend, Alexine Mangetout.'

Culculine made the introductions very gravely in a
luxurious boudoir decorated with obscene Japanese
prints.

The two friends kissed each other, using their tongues.
Both women were tall, but not excessively so.

Culculine was dark, her grey eyes flashed with malice
and a beauty spot with a little tuft of hair on it graced the
bottom of her left cheek. Her complexion was matt, the
blood coursed beneath her skin, her cheeks and forehead
wrinkled frequently, attesting to her preoccupation with
money and love.

Alexine was a blonde of that particular shade tending
towards ash which one sees only in Paris. Her complexion
was clear, almost transparent. In her charming rose-
coloured négligé, this pretty girl looked as dainty and as
roguish as a naughty eighteenth-century marchioness.

The formal introductions were soon over and Alexine,
who had had a Roumanian lover, went into her bedroom
to fetch his photograph. The prince and Culculine followed her. The pair threw themselves at her and laugh-

ingly undressed her. Her peignoir fell off, leaving her in a batiste chemise which revealed a charmingly buxom body, dimpled in the appropriate places.

Mony and Culculine tumbled her over on to the bed and exposed her lovely rosy tits, which were large and hard. Mony sucked the nipples. Culculine bent down and lifted her chemise, uncovering strong round thighs which met beneath a pussy of the same ash blonde as the hair of her head. Gurgling with pleasure, Alexine drew her little feet up on to the bed, letting her slippers fall to the floor with a sharp slap. Her legs spread wide, she lifted her arse to meet her friend's licking tongue and clasped her hands around Mony's neck.

It was not long before the desired result was achieved, her buttocks clenched, her body lashed more violently. Then she came, crying out:

'Beasts! You have excited me, now you must satisfy me.'

'He has sworn to do it twenty times!' said Culculine, taking off her clothes.

The prince followed her example. At the same moment each of them stood naked, admiring the other's body while Alexine lay swooning on the bed. Culculine's large bottom swayed deliciously below a very narrow waist. She grabbed hold of Mony's enormous prick, swelling over a huge pair of balls.

'Give it to her,' she said, 'you can do it to me afterwards.'

As the prince's member approached Alexine's half-open cunt, the girl trembled in anticipation:

'You'll kill me!' she cried.

But the prick sank in right up to the balls and was withdrawn and rammed in again like a piston. Culculine climbed on to the bed and laid her black bush on Alexine's mouth, while Mony licked her arsehole. Alexine moved her bottom like a woman possessed, she put one finger up Mony's arsehole and this caress made his cock still harder. He moved his hands round under Alexine's buttocks, while she clenched them together with unbelievable strength, gripping Mony's prick in her inflamed cunt in such a stranglehold that he could scarcely move.

Soon the three of them were thrashing about in a transport, panting and gasping. Alexine came three times, then it was Culculine's turn. Immediately afterwards, she moved down to nibble Mony's balls. Alexine began to cry out like a damned soul and when Mony shot his Roumanian spunk into her belly, she writhed like a serpent. Culculine at once wrenched him out of the hole and her mouth took the place of his cock, lapping up the sperm which was dribbling out in large droplets. Meanwhile, Alexine had taken Mony's weapon into her mouth and licked it clean, giving him a new erection at the same time.

A minute later, the prince threw himself on Culculine, but his prick remained at the entrance, titillating her clitoris. He seized one of the young woman's breasts in his mouth. Alexine caressed them both.

'Put it in,' cried Culculine, 'I can't bear it any longer.'

But his prick still lingered outside. She came twice, and was on the point of desperation when suddenly he penetrated her, right up to the womb. Wild with excitement and voluptuous delight, she bit Mony's ear so hard that a piece of it came away in her mouth. She swallowed it, shouting at the top of her voice and heaving her arse majestically. This wound, gushing with blood, seemed to excite Mony, for he began to plough her with increased vigour and did not leave Culculine's cunt until he had discharged three times, while she herself came ten times.

When he withdrew, they found to their amazement that Alexine had disappeared. She soon came back carrying pharmaceutical preparations for dressing Mony's ear and a huge coachman's whip.

'I bought this for 50 francs,' she exclaimed. 'I got it from the driver of Hackney-Carriage No. 3269, it will help us to make the Roumanian hard again. Let him bandage his ear, Culculine my love, while we do 69 to stimulate him.'

While he was staunching the blood, Mony watched the provocative spectacle of Culculine and Alexine, head to tail, greedily licking one another. Alexine's large backside, white and dimpled, dangled over Culculine's face; their tongues, as long as little boys' cocks, worked steadily, saliva and vaginal juices mingled, wet hairs stuck together and sighs – which would have been heart-rending if they had not been sighs of love – rose from the bed as it creaked and squeaked beneath the agreeable weight of the two pretty creatures.

'Come and bugger me!' cried Alexine.

But Mony was losing so much blood that he no longer had the strength to get an erection. Alexine stood up and, seizing the whip from Hackney-Carriage No. 3269, a superb brand new *perpignan,* brandished it and set about lashing Mony over the back and buttocks. Under the onslaught of this new pain, he forgot his bleeding ear and started to yell, but the naked Alexine, like a frenzied bacchante, kept on striking.

'Come and beat me too!' she cried to Culculine, who, with blazing eyes, began to thump Alexine's large, quivering arse as hard as she could. Soon Culculine was as excited as her friend.

'Beat me, Mony!' she pleaded, and the prince who was growing accustomed to the flagellation, although it had already drawn blood, started to slap her handsome, dusky buttocks, which opened and shut rhythmically. By the time his cock was stiff, the blood was flowing not only from his ear but from every weal left by the cruel whip.

Alexine then turned round and proffered her lovely reddened arse to the enormous prick, which pierced her little rosebud, while she, impaled, cried out, wriggling her backside and shaking her tits. But Culculine laughed and separated them, so that she and Alexine could resume their game of 69. Mony, streaming with blood, again buried his weapon up to the hilt in Alexine's arse and buggered her so vigorously that she was soon over-whelmed with joy. His balls swung to and fro like the bells of Notre-Dame and bounced against Culculine's nose. At a certain moment, Alexine squeezed her arsehole so tightly around the root of Mony's prick that he could no longer move. Then he came, his sperm sucked out in long jets by Alexine Mangetout's avid anus.

Meanwhile, out in the street, a crowd had gathered round Hackney-Carriage No. 3269, whose driver had no whip.

A policeman asked him what he had done with it.

'I sold it to a lady in rue Duphot.'

'Then go and get it back or I'll fine you.'

'All right, I'll go,' said the coachman, a Norman of exceptional strength. He asked the concierge for direc-tions, then rang the bell on the first floor.

Alexine answered the doorbell stark naked; the coach-man's eyes nearly started out of his head and when she fled into the bedroom he ran after her, caught hold of her and thrust a respectably-sized cock into her from the rear. He soon climaxed, shouting: 'Hell's bells, heaven's brothel and the Whore of Babylon!'

Alexine jerked her arse against him and came at the same moment, while Mony and Culculine were splitting their sides with mirth. The coachman, thinking they were laughing at him, flew into a terrible rage.

'Ugh, you whores, pimps, vultures, sewer rats, you're taking the piss out of me! My whip, where's my whip?'

And, catching sight of it, he snatched it up and began to flay Mony, Alexine and Culculine with all his might. Their naked bodies flinched under the blows which left bloody stripes. Then, his cock swelling again, he pounced on Mony and buggered him.

The front door had been left open and the police sergeant, tired of waiting for the coachman to return, had come in search of him, and it was at this precise moment that he entered the bedroom. Without wasting a moment, he pulled out his regulation-size prick and slipped it into Culculine's backside; she clucked like a hen and shivered at the cold contact of his uniform buttons.

Alexine, left to herself, took the white truncheon from its holster at the policeman's side. She inserted it into her cunt and soon all five of them were enjoying themselves immensely, while the blood from their wounds ran down on to the carpets, the sheets and the furniture and while, outside, the abandoned Hackney-Carriage No. 3269 was being led away to the police pound. The horse farted all the way, filling the street with a nauseating stench.

Chapter 3

It took Prince Vibescu several days to recover from the excitements of the bizarre session in which the policeman and the driver of Hackney-Carriage No. 3269 had so fortuitously joined. The weals left by the flagellation had now formed scars, and he was stretched out languorously on a sofa in his drawing-room at the Grand Hotel. To stimulate himself, he was reading various tit-bits from *Le Journal*. One story intrigued him. It was a hideous crime. A washer-up in a restaurant had roasted the backside of a young kitchen-hand, then he had buggered him, still hot and bleeding, at the same time eating the well-done morsels which fell away from the ephebe's posterior. Hearing the howls of the budding Vatel,* neighbours had rushed in and put a stop to the sadistic antics. The story was recounted in all its details, and the prince savoured every one, gently stroking his massive tool.

At that moment someone knocked at the door. The prince called 'Come in', and a vivacious chambermaid, utterly captivating in her cap and apron, entered the room. She was holding a letter and, when she saw Mony's unbuttoned state, she blushed. Doing up his flies, he said:

'Don't go, my pretty little blonde, I want a word with you.'

At the same time he closed the door and, seizing the charming Mariette round the waist, kissed her passionately on the mouth. At first she struggled and clamped her lips tightly together, but soon, in his strong embrace,

---

* Vatel (1635-1671) was a celebrated maitre d'hotel. It was his death that made him a legend : he stabbed himself to death when a shortage in the kitchens prevented him from serving the fish course on time to Louis XIV.

she relaxed and her mouth opened. The prince's tongue darted in to be bitten at once by Mariette, while her mobile tongue tickled the tip of Mony's.

With one hand, the young man encircled her waist, with the other he lifted her skirts. She was not wearing knickers. His hand soon slid in between two thighs which were larger and rounder than he would have expected, as she was tall and slim. Her cunt was very hairy. She was hot and excited and his hand soon found the moist slit. Abandoning herself, Mariette thrust her belly forward. Her hand strayed to his flies and she managed to unbutton them. She drew out the superb plaything which she had only glimpsed as she came in. They masturbated each other gently, he squeezing her clitoris, she pressing her thumb on the orifice of his glans. He pushed her back on to the sofa and she fell in a sitting position. He raised her legs and placed them on his shoulders, Mariette unfastened her bodice and two splendid tits popped out; Mony began to suck the erect nipples, each in turn, while he drove his flaming sword into her cunt. Soon she began to cry out:

'It's so good . . . ah, that's lovely . . . you're doing it so well. . . .'

Her buttocks rocked in total abandon, then he felt her coming as she said:

'There! . . . I'm coming . . . now . . . take it all!'

Immediately afterwards, she grabbed hold of his weapon:

'That's enough for pussy.'

And she pulled it out of her cunt and slid it into another hole, perfectly round, lower down, a Cyclops' eye between two cool, white, fleshy cheeks. Mony's prick, lubricated by her love-juice, penetrated easily and, after buggering her vigorously, he left all his sperm in the pretty chambermaid's arse. As he drew out his cock, it went 'pop' just as when one uncorks a bottle. There was still some spunk, mingled with a little shit, clinging to the tip of it. At that moment, a bell in the corridor rang and Mariette said: 'I must go and see to it.' She kissed Mony, who placed two *louis* in her hand, and ran out. As soon as she had gone, he washed his member, then tore open the letter which read as follows:

My handsome Roumanian,

What has become of you? Surely you have recovered from your labours by now. And remember your promise to me: *'If I do not make love to you twenty times in succession, may I be punished by eleven thousand scourges.'* Well, you did not do it twenty times – so much the worse for you.

The other day, I took you to Alexine's love-nest on the rue Duphot, but now that we are acquainted, you can come to my house. It is impossible to go to Alexine's, her senator is so jealous that she cannot even receive me there. That is why she keeps a love-nest. As for me, I don't give a damn – my lover is an explorer, at the moment he is away stringing pearls with the negresses on the Ivory Coast. We shall expect you at my place, 214, rue de Prony, at four o'clock.

Culculine d'Ancône.

As soon as he had read this letter, the prince looked at the time. It was eleven in the morning. He rang for the masseur, who massaged him and buggered him dexterously. This session revived his spirits. After he had bathed, feeling fresh and in the right mood, he rang for the hairdresser, who set his hair and buggered him artistically. Then the manicurist-pedicurist came up. He did the prince's nails and buggered him vigorously. Then Mony felt completely relaxed. He went down, walked along the boulevards, ate a copious lunch and hailed a cab to take him to the rue de Prony. It was a small town-house, occupied solely by Culculine. An old maidservant let him in. The place was furnished in exquisite taste.

He was shown straight into a bedroom with a very low, and very wide, brass bed. The parquet flooring was strewn with animal pelts which muffled the sound of footsteps. The prince undressed quickly and was already stark naked when Alexine and Culculine came in, wearing the most ravishing négligés. They laughed and kissed him. He sat down, taking one of the young women on each knee and lifting up their skirts in such a way that they remained decently covered yet he could feel their bare bottoms on his thighs. Then he began to titillate them, with one hand each, while they tickled his prick. When he felt that they were growing hot with excitement, he said:

'Now we shall begin our lesson.'

He made them sit down on chairs facing him and, after a moment's reflection, said to them:

'*Mesdemoiselles,* I have just discovered that you are not wearing knickers. You should be ashamed of yourselves. Go and put them on at once.'

When they came back, he resumed the lesson.

'Mademoiselle Alexine Mangetout, what is the name of the King of Italy?'

'I haven't the faintest idea,' said Alexine, 'anyway, who cares?'

'Go and get on the bed!' shouted the schoolmaster.

He made her kneel on the bed with her back towards him, then lift her skirts and part the slit in her knickers. As she did so, the dazzling white globes of her buttocks appeared. He started slapping her with the flat of his hand; soon the cheeks of her posterior were blushing. This excited Alexine, who thrust her arse out eagerly, and before long the prince could no longer restrain himself. Passing his hands round the young woman's bust, he seized hold of her breasts through the négligé, then, sliding one hand downward, he tickled her clitoris and felt that her cunt was quite wet.

Her hands were not idle: she had seized the prince's weapon and directed it into the narrow path of Sodom. Alexine bent forward to make her arse protrude and facilitate the entry of Mony's prick.

Soon the glans was inside, the rest followed and the balls came thudding against the base of the girl's buttocks. Culculine, not wanting to be left out, also climbed on to the bed and began to lick Alexine's vulva. Thus pleasured and fêted from both sides, the latter was ready to weep with joy. Her body shuddered with sensual delight, she writhed as if in pain, and voluptuous gurgles escaped from her throat. The huge horn filled her back passage and, thrusting to and fro, beat against the membrane that separated it from Culculine's tongue, which licked up the juices produced by this pleasant pastime. Mony's abdomen pounded against Alexine's arse. Soon the prince's buggering movements became even stronger. He began biting the young woman's neck. His weapon swelled to bursting. Alexine could no longer bear so much pleasure, she sank down on to the face of Culculine, who never ceased her licking, while the prince, his cock embedded in her arse, collapsed on top of her. A few more jerks of the loins, then Mony let go his spunk. She lay stretched out on the bed while Mony went to wash himself and Culculine got up to piss. She took a bowl, stood over it with her legs astride, lifted her skirt and pissed copiously, then, to blow away the last drops that were dangling in her pubic hair, she let out a discreet and delicate little fart, which considerably excited Mony.

'Shit in my hands!' he cried. 'Shit in my hands!'

She smiled. He crouched behind her while she lowered her arse a little and began to strain. She was wearing a pair of knickers made of transparent batiste; through them could be seen her marvellously lithe thighs. Black lace stockings came up above her knees and moulded two superb calves of incomparable contour, neither too fat nor too thin. In her present position, her rump stood out, admirably framed by the slit in the knickers. Mony's eyes were riveted to the two brown and rosy buttocks, dimpled here and there and animated by a generous flow of blood. He observed that the base of the dorsal spine was somewhat prominent, and the crack between the buttocks started immediately below it, wide at first, then narrowing and becoming deeper as the cheeks reached their maximum fullness; thus one arrived at the brown, round arsehole, tightly pleated. At first, the young woman's efforts had the effect of dilating the arsehole and making the little ring of smooth pink skin, which is found in the interior, protrude like a curled lip.

'Come on, shit!' cried Mony.

Soon the tip of a turd appeared, pointed and insignificant, but it retreated instantly into its cavern. It showed its head again, followed slowly and majestically by the rest of the sausage which constituted one of the finest turds a large intestine has ever produced.

The shit slipped out, unctuously and without interruption, paying out steadily like the cable of a ship. It dangled gracefully between the pretty buttocks, which opened wider and wider apart. Soon it was swinging more vigorously. The arse dilated still further, shook itself a little and the shit fell, all hot and steaming, into Mony's outstretched and eager hands. Then he cried: 'Don't move!' and, bending down, licked her arsehole thoroughly whilst rolling the turd between his hands. Next, he crushed it voluptuously and smeared it all over his body. Culculine undressed, following the example of Alexine, who was now stark naked and showing her large backside, which had the transparent complexion of a blonde, to Mony. 'Shit on me!' he ordered Alexine, and stretched out on the floor. She squatted over him, but not too low, so that he could enjoy the full view of her arsehole. Her first efforts did no more than force out a little of the spunk Mony had deposited there; then came the shit, yellow and soft, which fell in several pieces and, as she laughed and wriggled her arse, these turds fell here and there, scattered all over Mony's body. His belly was soon adorned with several odoriferous slugs.

Alexine had pissed at the same time and the hot jet, falling on Mony's prick, had reawakened his animal spirits. His quill began to rise up, swelling little by little till it reached its normal size and the gland, as red as a ripe plum, stood erect under the gaze of the young woman who, lowering her body, crouching more and more, guided the rampant prick in between the velvety lips of her gaping cunt. Mony revelled in the spectacle. Alexine's arse, as it descended, displayed its appetizing rotundity ever more clearly, the roundness becoming more pronounced and the spreading of the buttocks more accentuated. When her rump had come right down and completely swallowed his cock, she raised it up again and her arse began a delightful up-and-down motion which modified its volume and its essential proportions, providing Mony with the most delectable show. The prince, covered in shit, was wallowing in a profound pleasure. Soon, he felt her vagina contract and Alexine said in a strangled voice: 'Swine! I'm coming . . . I'm coming!' and she spilled her love-juice. But Culculine, who had been watching this operation and seemed like a bitch on heat, pulled her roughly off the stake that impaled her and, unconcerned about the shit on Mony's body sullying her too, threw herself on him and slid his weapon into her cunt with a sigh of satisfaction. She began riding him ferociously, saying with each thrust of her loins: 'Hah!' Alexine, angry at being robbed of her spoil, opened a drawer and pulled out a strap made of leather thongs. She began thrashing Culculine's arse, making her jerk her body still more frenziedly. Alexine, excited by this sight, struck hard and true. Blows rained on the superb posterior. By leaning his head a little to one side, Mony could see, in a mirror opposite him, Culculine's plump arse rising and falling. As the buttocks rose, they half-opened and the rosebud appeared for an instant to disappear on the descent when the splendid full-blown cheeks squeezed together again. Below them, the hairy and distended lips of her cunt swallowed up the enormous prick which, during the rising motion, appeared almost in its entire length and glistening wet. Alexine's blows had crimsoned the poor backside which now bounced and shivered with voluptuous delight. Soon, one blow left a bleeding weal. Both the women, the one who was wielding the whip and her victim, were as delirious as Bacchantes and seemed to derive equal pleasure from the exercise. Mony himself began to partake of their fury and his nails dug into Culculine's satiny back. To strike at Culculine more comfortably, Alexine knelt down beside the pair. Her big fleshy backside, shuddering as she delivered each blow, was only an inch or two from Mony's mouth.

His tongue soon found the crack, then, in the fury of his voluptuous rage, he started biting her right buttock. The girl cried out in pain. His teeth had penetrated the skin and a fresh, vermilion blood spurted out to quench Mony's parched throat. He lapped it up, savouring the strong, slightly salty taste of iron. At this moment, Culculine's bouncing movements became utterly abandoned. Her upturned eyes showed nothing but the whites. Her mouth stained with shit from Mony's body, she let out a groan and came at the same time as he did. Alexine fell across them, exhausted, grinding her teeth and making a sound like a death-rattle in her throat. Mony put his mouth to her cunt and had only to ply his tongue two or three times to bring her to orgasm. After several shuddering convulsions, their nerves relaxed and the trio lay sprawled in the shit, the blood and the sperm. They fell asleep in this position and when they awoke the bedroom clock was just chiming the twelve strokes of midnight.

'Don't move,' said Culculine, 'I heard a noise. It can't be my maid, she always keeps out of the way. Anyway, she must be in bed by now.'

A cold sweat broke out on Mony's and the girls' foreheads. Their hair stood on end and shivers ran through their nude and shit-stained bodies.

'There's someone there,' said Alexine.

'Yes, there's someone there,' Mony agreed.

At that moment the door opened and the glimmer of light that filtered in from the nocturnal street allowed them to make out two human shadows dressed in overcoats with the collars turned up and wearing bowler hats on their heads.

Suddenly, the first man switched on an electric torch which he was holding in his hand. The beam lit up the room, but at first the burglars did not notice the group lying on the floor.

'What a stink!' said the first man.

'Never mind that, let's go in, there must be some swag in the drawers,' replied the other.

Meanwhile, Culculine had crawled towards the light switch; suddenly, she flooded the room with light.

The burglars were dumbfounded at the sight of all this nudity.

'Christ Almighty!' said the first, 'you've got nice habits, and it's Cornabœux who says so!'

He was a swarthy colossus with hairy paws. A bushy beard made his face even more repulsive.

'What a farce!' said the second, 'as for me, I like shit, it's lucky.'

He was a pale-faced, shifty-looking scoundrel with one eye; he was chewing on a lighted fag-end.

'Yer'right, La Chaloupe,' said Cornabœux, 'I've just trodden in some and I think, for my first bit of luck, I'm going to poke mademoiselle there. But first, let's take care of the bloke.'

And throwing themselves upon the terrified Mony, the burglars gagged him and bound him hand and foot. Then, turning to the two women, who were shivering yet somewhat amused by the turn of events, La Chaloupe said:

'And you, my poppets, try and be nice to us, eh? Or I'll have to tell your Daddy.'

He was holding a cane in his hand; giving it to Culculine, he ordered her to thrash Mony with all her strength. Then, placing himself behind her, he brought out a cock as thin as a little finger, but very long. Culculine was beginning to enjoy the situation. La Chaloupe started by slapping her on the buttocks.

'Now then,' he said, 'these two lovely chubby cheeks are going to play the flute, I'm going to stick it up the Khyber pass.'

He stroked and fondled her plump, downy bottom and, passing one hand round to the front, manipulated her clitoris, then, abruptly, he inserted his long skinny weapon. Culculine began to rotate her arse, at the same time beating Mony who, unable to defend himself or cry out, wriggled like a worm at each blow of the cane, which left red marks that soon turned purple. As the buggery excited her more and more, Culculine struck harder and harder, shouting:

'Swine! Filthy beast, take that, and that! . . . La Chaloupe, drive your little toothpick in, all the way.'

Soon Mony's body was streaming with blood.

Meanwhile, Cornabœux had seized hold of Alexine and thrown her down on to the bed. He nibbled at her nipples, which began to harden. Then he moved down to her fanny, taking the whole organ into his mouth, while he pulled at the pretty blonde curls of her bush. He stood up again and took out a short but enormously thick

cock with a violet knob. Turning Alexine over, he started
slapping her large pink arse; from time to time, he passed
his hand down the crack. Then he took the young woman
on his left arm in such a way that his right hand could
get at her cunt. The left hand still held her by the hairs
of her bush . . . which hurt her. She cried out and her
moans grew louder as Cornabœux began slapping her
again with all his might. Her strong rosy thighs jigged
up and down and her arse quivered every time the burglar's huge paw struck. At last, she tried to defend herself;
her little hands scratched at the bearded face. She pulled
his facial hair as hard as he was pulling her pubic hair.

'That's enough of that,' said Cornabœux and turned
her over.

At that moment she caught sight of La Chaloupe, who
was buggering Culculine who was beating Mony who was
already bathed in blood, and the spectacle excited her.
Cornabœux's huge prick rammed against her behind,
but he missed his mark, thumping to the right or left,
above or below. When he found the hole, he placed his
hands on Alexine's plump and gleaming haunches and
pulled her towards him with all his strength. His enormous prick tore her arsehole, and she would have cried
out in pain if she had not been so carried away by all that
had just taken place. As soon as he had driven his cock
into her arse, Cornabœux took it out again, then, rolling
Alexine over on the bed, he forced his instrument into
her front passage. Due to its size, the mighty weapon penetrated with difficulty, but as soon as it was in Alexine
crossed her legs over the burglar's hips and kept them so
tightly locked that he could not have withdrawn even if
he had wanted to. They fucked furiously. Cornabœux
sucked her titties and his beard tickled and excited her,
she slipped one hand inside his trousers and inserted a
finger in the burglar's arsehole. Then they began biting
one another like wild beasts, thrashing their loins at the

same time. They reached a frenzied orgasm. But Cornabœux's penis, strangled by Alexine's vagina, began to stiffen again immediately. Alexine closed her eyes, the better to savour this second swelling erection. She came fourteen times, while Cornabœux came three times. When she recovered her senses, she saw that both her cunt and her arse were bleeding, wounded by Cornabœux's gigantic prick. She glanced at Mony, who was writhing convulsively on the floor.

His body was one huge sore.

Culculine, on orders from the villainous La Chaloupe, was kneeling before him and sucking his cock.

'Come on, on your feet, you bitch!' shouted Cornabœux.

Alexine obeyed and he gave her a kick on the arse which sent her sprawling on top of Mony. Ignoring her supplications, Cornabœux tied her arms and legs and gagged her, then, seizing the cane, he began to beat her slender but well-rounded body till it was covered in stripes. Her bottom flinched at each blow of the stick, then her back, her belly, her thighs, her breasts received the onslaught of the attack. Writhing and struggling, Alexine's body struck against Mony's prick, which was as rigid as a corpse's. By chance, this weapon encountered the young woman's cunt and penetrated.

Cornabœux redoubled his blows, striking indiscriminately at Mony and Alexine who derived a fiendish joy from their pain. Soon the girl's delicate, rosy skin had become invisible beneath the weals and the flowing blood. Mony had already fainted, and she fainted soon afterwards. Cornabœux, whose arm was growing tired, turned towards Culculine, who was still trying to bring La Chaloupe to a climax. But, in spite of its load, the villain's weapon refused to discharge.

Cornabœux ordered the beautiful raven-haired girl to spread her thighs. He had a good deal of trouble in penetrating her from the rear. She suffered, but stoically, never for a moment letting go of La Chaloupe's cock, which she was still sucking. Once Cornabœux had taken full possession of Culculine's cunt, he raised her right arm and chewed the hairs in her armpit, where she had a very dense mop. When Culculine reached her orgasm, the pleasure was so intense that she fainted, at the same time clamping her teeth together violently on La Chaloupe's prick. He gave a terrible scream of pain, but the gland had been bitten clean off. Cornabœux, who had just ejaculated, abruptly withdrew his broad-sword from Culculine's cunt, letting her fall to the floor in a dead faint. La Chaloupe was bleeding like a stuck pig.

'My poor La Chaloupe,' said Cornabœux, 'you're done for, fucked. Might as well hand in your chips right now.' And, pulling out a knife, he struck La Chaloupe a mortal blow, at the same time shaking the last drops of spunk that clung to his cock over the postrate form of Culculine. La Chaloupe died without a murmur.

Cornabœux dressed again at his leisure, emptied all the money and clothing from the drawers and took all the watches and jewellery. Then he looked at Culculine, lying on the floor in a swoon.

'I must avenge La Chaloupe,' he thought and, drawing out his knife once more, he struck a terrible blow between Culculine's buttocks. The girl remained unconscious. Cornabœux left his dagger sticking in her arse. The clocks struck three a.m. Then he departed the way he had come, leaving four bodies stretched out on the floor of the room – a room that was full of blood, shit, spunk and indescribable chaos.

Out in the street, he turned his steps cheerfully towards Ménilmontant, singing:

> An arse should stink like an arse
> And not like eau de Cologne. . . .

and then :

> Gassssssss . . . jet,
> Gasssssssss . . . jet,
> Light up my little wick. . . .

Chapter 4

The affair caused a terrific scandal; the newspapers were full of it for a week. Culculine, Alexine and Prince Vibescu were confined to their beds for two months. One evening, when Mony was convalescing, he went into a bar near the gare Montparnasse. The speciality of the house was paraffin, a delectable drink for palates jaded with the more ordinary liqueurs.

As he was imbibing the notorious rot-gut, the prince studied the customers. One of them, a bearded Titan, was dressed like a porter from Les Halles and his huge hat, sprinkled with flour, lent him the air of a fabulous demi-god about to perform some heroic labour.

The prince felt almost sure it was that engaging burglar, Cornabœux. Suddenly, he heard him demand a glass of paraffin in a thunderous voice. It was indeed the voice of Cornabœux. Mony stood up and walked towards him with his hand outstretched.

'Good evening, Cornabœux, are you working at Les Halles now?'

'Me?' said the astonished porter. 'How the devil do you know me?'

'Oh,' said Mony with a nonchalant air, 'I met you at number 214, rue de Prony.'

'It wasn't me,' said Cornabœux, taking fright. 'I don't know you. I've been a porter at Les Halles for three years, ask anyone, they all know me. Leave me alone.'

'Don't talk nonsense,' replied Mony. 'You are mine, Cornabœux. I could hand you over to the police, but I have taken a liking to you. If you wish to follow me, I will make you my valet de chambre. You will go everywhere

with me and join me in all my pleasures. You will assist
me and, when necessary, protect me. Then, if you prove
faithful, I shall make your fortune for you. I want your
answer at once.'

'You're a decent bloke and you know how to talk to a
fellow. Right, done! I'm your man.'

A few days later, Cornabœux, promoted to the rank of
valet de chambre, was strapping up the suitcases. Prince
Mony had been recalled to Bucharest on urgent business.
His intimate friend, the Serbian Vice-Consul, had just
died, leaving the major part of his worldly goods to him.
These consisted of tin mines, which had been very pro-
ductive for a number of years but now needed personal
supervision at close quarters, otherwise there was a dan-
ger of a serious decline in output. As has been seen, Prince
Mony had no love of money for its own sake, but he
desired to be as rich as possible so as to indulge in the
pleasures that gold can purchase. He was constantly quoting a maxim pronounced by one of his ancestors: 'Everything is for sale, everything can be bought; it is merely a
question of the price.'

Prince Mony and Cornabœux had booked seats on the
Orient Express. The vibration of the train did not fail to
have an immediate effect: Mony had a horn on him like
a Cossack stallion and kept throwing impassioned glances
at Cornabœux. Beyond the window, the admirable landscape of eastern France unfurled its neat and tranquil
splendours. The saloon-car was almost empty; a gouty
old fellow, richly-attired, was whimpering and slobbering
over the *Figaro* he was attempting to read.

Mony, who was clad in a loose-fitting raglan coat, seized
Cornabœux's hand and, pushing it through the slit which
opened in the pocket of this ample garment, guided it to
his fly-buttons. The colossal valet de chambre understood
his master's wishes. His huge hand bristled with hairs,
but it was plump and gentler than one would have imag-

ined. Cornabœux's fingers delicately unbuttoned the prince's trousers. He seized the ecstatic prick which, on all points, justified Alphonse Allais' famous couplet:

> The titillating motion of trains
> Sends desire coursing all through our veins.

However, just then, an employee of the Compagnie des Wagons-Lits came in to announce that it was time for dinner and the dining-car was already filling up with passengers.

'An excellent idea,' said Mony. 'Come along, Cornabœux, let us dine first.'

The ex-market porter removed his hand from the slit in the prince's overcoat. They walked through to the dining-car. The latter's cock was still erect and, since he had not troubled to button himself up again, there was a marked protuberance on the front of the garment. Dinner began comfortably, cradled by the clattering of the train and the various clinking and chinking of china, silverware and glass. Now and then, it was disturbed by the abrupt pop of an *Apollinaris* cork.

At the opposite end of the dining-car, two attractive, fair-haired women were sitting at a table. Cornabœux, who was facing them, pointed them out to Mony. The prince turned round and recognized the more modestly-dressed of the two: it was Mariette, the exquisite chambermaid from the Grand Hotel. Immediately, he stood up and approached the ladies. He greeted Mariette and addressed himself to the other young woman, whose pretty face was heavily made up. Her peroxide blonde hair gave her a daringly modern look which Mony found quite ravishing.

'Madame,' he said to her, 'I beg you to forgive my presumption. I take the liberty of introducing myself only because it would be difficult to find common acquaintances on this train. I am Prince Mony Vibescu, hereditary Hospodar. Allow me to explain that I have incurred a debt of gratitude towards this young lady here, Mademoiselle Mariette, who, I take it, has left the Grand Hotel and is now in your service. I intend to discharge the debt this very day. I wish to marry her to my valet de chambre, and I shall bestow a dowry of 50,000 francs upon each of them.'

'I see no obstacle to your plan,' said the lady, 'but I see something there which appears to be rather well-endowed. On whom is it to be bestowed?'

Mony's cock had found an outlet and its rubicund head was peeping out between two buttons. The prince blushed as he tucked the weapon out of sight. The lady was seized with laughter.

'Fortunately, you were standing in such a position that nobody could have seen . . . otherwise there might have been a fine to-do. . . . But, tell me, who is to be the beneficiary of this redoubtable equipment?'

'Permit me,' said Mony gallantly, 'to offer it as a tribute to your sovereign beauty.'

'Well, we shall see about that,' said the lady. 'Meanwhile, since you have introduced yourself, I shall do the same . . . Estelle Ronange. . . .'

'The great actress from the *Comédie française*?' asked Mony.

The lady bowed her head.

Overwhelmed with joy, Mony exclaimed :

'Estelle! I should have recognized you. I have been a passionate admirer of yours for a long time. Have I not spent entire evenings at the theatre, watching you in your romantic roles? And to assuage my excitement, since I could hardly masturbate in public, I dug my fingers into my nose, picked out the solid snot and ate it ! It was good, oh, delicious !'

'Mariette, go and dine with your fiancé,' said Estelle.

'Prince you will dine with me.'

As soon as they were sitting facing one another, the prince and the actress exchanged amorous looks.

'Where are you going?' asked Mony.

'To Vienna, to act before the Emperor.'

'And the Moscow Decree?'*

'I don't give a damn for the Moscow Decree; tomorrow, I shall send Claretie my resignation. . . . They are putting me in the shade . . . making me play minor parts . . . they have refused me the role of Eoraka in Mounet-Sully's new play. . . . I am leaving. . . . I will not let them stifle my talent.'

'Recite something to me . . . some poetry,' begged Mony.

While the waiters were changing the plates, she recited *L'Invitation au Voyage* for him. As that admirable poem unfolded its beauties, a poem into which Baudelaire has instilled something of his amorous sorrow and his passionate nostalgia, Mony felt the actress's little feet sliding up his legs; underneath the raglan coat they reached his cock, which was dangling sadly out of his flies. There they stopped and, delicately grasping the weapon between them, began a rather curious up-and-down movement. The young man's cock hardened at once and allowed itself to be masturbated by Estelle Ronange's dainty slippers. Soon, he began to enjoy it and improvised this sonnet, which he recited to the actress, whose pedestrian efforts did not cease until the last verse:

---

*Dictated by Napoleon I in Moscow, and passed by the Conseil d'Etat on 15 October, 1812, the *Decret de Moscou* was the administrative statute of the *Comédie français*. It laid down the very strict rules and conditions governing performances by the *Sociétaires* on stages other than those of the *Comédie française*. It was still basically in force in 1904; thus, by appearing in Vienna, Estelle Ronange (Marguerite Moréno) would have been breaking her contract and forfeiting her privileges, pension, etc., as a member of the state theatre company.

EPITHALAMIUM

Your hands will guide my potent stallion's tool
Into the blessèd brothel agape between your thighs,
And I'll declare, in spite of Avinain,
I care not for your love, provided that you come!

My lips upon your breasts as white as cottage cheese
Will pay due homage with sweet strawberry bites,
And from my rampant cock into your female cleft
The sperm will gush like gold in the prospector's sluice.

Oh lovely, tender whore! Your buttocks distil
The mystic savour of Earth's fleshy fruits
And in form surpass the planet's merely sexless sphere,
Rounder than the moon, so vain of its rotundity,
And from your eyes, even when you veil them, spurts
That obscure clarity which tumbles from the stars.*

And as his prick had reached the limit of excitation,
Estelle lowered her feet, saying:

'My dear Prince, what would people think of us if we
let him spit in the dining-car? . . . I would like to thank
you for the homage you paid to Corneille in your sonnet.
Although I am about to leave the *Comédie française,*
everything concerning the company is still of vital
interest to me.'

'But what do you intend to do,' asked Mony, 'after you
have played before Franz-Josef?'

'It is my dream to become the star of a *café-concert,'*
said Estelle.

---

* The last line of the sonnet, '*Cette obscure clarté qui tombe des étoiles*',
is a splendid misapplication of a line from Corneille's *Le Cid.* Le Cid is
describing the Moorish fleet approaching the coast, where his own army is
waiting in ambush:

> *Cette obscure clarté qui tombe des étoiles*
> *Enfin avec le flux nous fait voir trente voiles;*
> *L'onde s'enfle dessous, et d'un commun effort*
> *Les Maures et la mer montent jusques au port.* . . .
>
> (*Le Cid*, Act IV, Scene iii, Line 1,273)

It is also, of course, a pun on 'Claretie' (see note on p. 12).

'Beware!' Mony retorted, 'the *obscure Monsieur
Claretie who tumbles the stars* will start endless lawsuits
against you.'

'Don't worry about that, Mony, make up some more
verses for me before we go beddy-byes.'

'Very well,' said Mony, and he improvised these exquisite mythological sonnets.

HERCULES AND OMPHALE

Omphale's
Bum
Overcome
Falls.

'Do you feel
My phallus
Like steel?'
– 'What balls! . . .

The dog
Has split
My arse.
– Oh, shit!' . . .

– . . . 'All right?
. . . Hold tight!'

On his knees
Hercules
Buggers
Omphale.

PYRAMUS AND THISBE

The lady
Thisbe
Swoons:
'Oh, baby!'

> Pyramus
> Amorous
> Croons:
> 'Oh, lady!'
>
> She bends
> Says: 'Ooh!'
> He rends
>
> Her bum
> She's come
> He too.

'That's exquisite! Delicious! Magnificent! Mony you are divine, an arch-poet, come and fuck me in the sleeping-car, my very soul is in the mood for love.'

Mony paid the bills. Mariette and Cornabœux were gazing languorously into each other's eyes. In the corridor, Mony slipped a 50 franc tip to the attendant and he let the two couples into the same sleeping-compartment:

'Fix things with the customs for us,' said the prince to the official, 'we have nothing to declare. Oh, and by the way, knock on our door two minutes before we reach the frontier.'

Once inside the compartment, all four stripped down to their birthday suits. Mariette was the first to be ready. Mony had never seen her in her naked state before, but he recognized her large round thighs and the forest of hair that flourished on her fleshy mound. Her nipples were as erect as Mony's and Cornabœux's pricks.

'Cornabœux,' said Mony, 'bugger me while I slip this pretty girl a length.'

Estelle took longer to undress and by the time she was naked Mony had already penetrated Mariette's cunt from behind; the girl was beginning to enjoy it, thrashing her large posterior about and making it slap against Mony's abdomen. Cornabœux had pressed his short, thick knob into the prince's dilated anus. Mony shouted:

'Confound this train! We won't be able to keep our balance.'

Mariette was clucking like a hen and tottering about as if she were tipsy. Mony had put his arms around her and was crushing her breasts. He admired the beauty of Estelle, whose coiffure revealed the hand of a skilled hairdresser. She was the last word in modern womanhood, with her waved hair held in place by tortoiseshell combs toning in colour with the subtle bleaching of the hair itself. Her body was charmingly pretty. Her lithe backside tilted at a provocative angle. Her face, made up with consummate art, lent her the titillating air of a very highclass prostitute. Her breasts were small, slender and pearshaped, they drooped a little, but this was most becoming to her. They were soft and silky to the touch; it was like fondling the udder of a nanny-goat; and, when she turned, they bounced like a batiste handkerchief rolled into a ball and juggled on the hand.

Her mound of Venus was covered with nothing but a little tuft of silky hair. She climbed on to the *couchette* and, with an agile movement, flung her long, sinewy thighs around Mariette's neck. Finding her mistress's quim in front of her face, Mariette began to gobble it greedily, pushing her nose in between the buttocks and into the arsehole. Estelle had already thrust her tongue into her maid's cunt and was sucking, at one and the same time, the interior of an inflamed fanny and Mony's huge prick, which was ardently ploughing it. Cornabœux gazed at this spectacle in a state of beatitude. His stout cock, buried to the hilt in the prince's hairy arse, moved slowly in and out. He let off two or three healthy farts which poisoned the atmosphere, increasing the delight of the prince and the two women. Suddenly Estelle started flinging herself about in the most frightful fashion, her arse began to dance in front of Mariette's nose and the girl responded by gurgling more loudly and wriggling her arse still more vigorously. Estelle's legs, sheathed in black silk and shod in slippers with Louis XV heels, lashed out to right and left. In the course of these convulsions, she kicked Cornabœux violently on the nose; he was stunned by the blow and began to bleed copiously. 'Whore!' he shouted and, in revenge, pinched Mony's arse viciously. The latter, seized with rage, bit Mariette's shoulder ferociously. Bellowing, the girl reached her orgasm, and, as a reaction to the pain, planted her teeth firmly in her mistress's cunt. Estelle became hysterical and squeezed her thighs together round Mariette's neck.

'I'm suffocating!' the maid managed to gasp, but they took no notice of her. The vice-like grip of Estelle's thighs tightened about her neck, her face turned purple, her mouth, flecked with foam, remained clenched on the actress's cunt.

With a yell, Mony ejaculated into an inert cunt. Cornabœux, with his eyes starting out of his head, spurted his spunk into Mony's arse, declaring in a faint voice:

'If that doesn't make you pregnant, you're not a man!'

The four people were spent and exhausted. Estelle was grinding her teeth, punching the air with her fists and waving her legs about. Cornabœux pissed out of the window. Mony was trying to withdraw his prick from Mariette's vagina. [. . .]

'Let me go,' Mony said to her; he caressed her, then pinched her buttocks and bit her, but there was no response.

'Come and prise her legs apart, she's fainted,' Mony said to Cornabœux.

It was only with the greatest difficulty that the prince managed to extract his cock from the ferociously tight cunt. [. . .]

'Shit! She's croaked!' exclaimed Cornabœux. [. . .], Mariette [. . .] was dead, irremediably dead.

'Now we're bitched!' said Mony.

'That dirty sow is the cause of it all,' declared Cornabœux, pointing to Estelle, who was beginning to calm
down. And, taking a hairbrush from the actress's vanity
case, he started to beat her violently with it. The bristles
stung her flesh at each blow. This chastisement seemed
to excite her tremendously.

At that moment, someone knocked at the door.

'The agreed signal,' said Mony, 'in a few moments, we
shall pass the frontier. I swore I would enjoy a screw,
half in France and half in Germany. We must do it. Shag
the corpse!'

Prick rampant, Mony threw himself upon Estelle, who
spread her thighs and received him in her burning cunt,
crying:

'Put it in, right in, there! ... ah!'

She jerked her arse with almost demonic frenzy, her
mouth drooled a saliva which, mixing with the make-up,
trickled uncleanly down her chin and neck. Mony slid
his tongue into her mouth and forced the handle of the
hairbrush up her arse. Under the impact of this new
voluptuous pleasure, she bit Mony's tongue so hard that
he had to pinch her to the point of drawing blood before
she would let go.

[... *]

'Infamous swine!' cried the prince. 'The rape of this
dead girl, whom I promised you would marry, will weigh
heavily against you in the Valley of Jehosophat. If I were
not so fond of you, I would kill you like a dog.'

Cornabœux stood up [...]. He pointed at Estelle,
whose dilated eyes contemplated the unspeakable scene
with horror.

'It's all her fault,' he declared.

---

* *Cornabœux has unnatural and violent intercourse with the dead Mariette.
Mony watches stupefied.*

'Do not be so cruel,' said Mony, 'it was she who gave you the chance to satisfy your necrophiliac lusts.'

As they were passing over a bridge, the prince went and stood at the window to contemplate the romantic panorama of the Rhine, which was unfurling its verdant splendours as it meandered in broad, sweeping curves as far as the horizon. It was four o'clock in the morning; cows were grazing in the meadows, children were already dancing beneath the Germanic linden trees. The sound of fife music, monotonous and funereal, announced the presence of a Prussian regiment, and this dirge mingled sadly with the clattering of the bridge and the heavy, thudding accompaniment of the moving train. Cheerful villages animated the river banks dominated by centenarian castles, and Rhenish vines laid out their regular and precious mosaic as far as the eye could see.

[. . . . *]
[. . . **]

'Now,' said Cornabœux, 'we must piss off out of here.'

They washed and dressed themselves, then climbed out of the carriage door and lay down daringly on the running-board of the train, which was hurtling along at full speed. At a signal from Cornabœux, they let themselves fall as gently as possible onto the ballast beside the rails. They picked themselves up, somewhat shaken but unharmed, and with a deliberate and ironic gesture saluted the train which was already dwindling into the distance.

'Not a moment too soon!' said Mony.

On reaching the nearest town, they rested there for two days, then reboarded the train for Bucharest.

The double murder on the Orient Express gave the

---

* *Cornabœux kills Estelle with a knife.*
**Mony makes love to the dying woman.*

newspapers copy for six months. The assassins were not found, so the crime was laid at the door of Jack the Ripper, as convenient a scapegoat as any.

In Bucharest, Mony collected his inheritance from the Serbian Vice-Consul. Since he was on good terms with the Serbian colony, he received an invitation to spend an evening at the home of Natasha Kolowić, wife of a colonel who had been imprisoned for his opposition to the Obrenović dynasty.

Mony and Cornabœux arrived about eight o'clock. The beautiful Natasha was in a drawing-room hung with black drapes, lit by yellow candles and decorated with the skulls and leg-bones of the dead.

'Prince Vibescu,' said the lady, 'you are about to witness a secret session of the anti-dynastic committee of Serbia. Tonight, we shall undoubtedly vote for the assassination of the infamous Alexander and his whore of a wife, Draga Mašin; it is our intention to reinstate the king, Peter Karadjordjević, on the throne of his ancestors. If you disclose what you are about to see and hear, an invisible hand will seek you out and kill you, no matter where you may be.'

Mony and Cornabœux bowed. The conspirators arrived one by one. André Bar, the Parisian journalist, was the moving spirit of the plot. He arrived, looking sinister and funereal, enveloped in a Spanish-style cape.

The conspirators stripped off their clothing and the lovely Natasha displayed her nudity in all its magnificence. Her backside gleamed and her belly was invisible beneath a black, curly bush that came right up to her navel.

She lay down on a table covered with a black sheet. A priest entered, dressed in sacerdotal vestments. He arranged the sacred vessels and began to say mass on Natasha's belly. Mony was standing close to Natasha; she seized his cock and sucked it throughout the course of the

mass. Cornabœux threw himself on André Bar and buggered him while the latter made a lyrical speech :

'I swear by this enormous prick which is pleasuring me
to the depths of my soul that the Obrenović dynasty will
be extinguished before long. Shove it in, Cornabœux!
Your buggering is giving me a cock-stand.'

Placing himself behind Mony, he buggered him while
the prince discharged his spunk into the mouth of the
beautiful Natasha. Roused by this sight, all the conspirators began buggering one another in a frenzy. In the
whole of that room there was nothing to be seen but the
vigorous arses of men impaled on formidable weapons.

The priest made Natasha toss him off twice and his
ecclesiastical spunk spouted over the body of the beautiful colonel's wife.

'Let the bride and groom be brought in,' cried the
priest.

A strange little couple were ushered in : a small boy of
ten, wearing a suit and with an opera hat under his arm,
accompanied by a ravishing little girl no older than eight;
she was dressed as a bride, her white satin dress adorned
with sprigs of orange blossom.

The priest read a sermon and married them by an
exchange of rings. Then the pair were set to fornicating.
The little boy pulled out a tool no bigger than a little
finger, and the new bride, hoisting up her frilly skirts,
exposed her dainty white thighs, with a little hairless cleft
gaping at the top, as pink as the inside of a new-born jay's
beak. A religious silence hovered over the assembly. The
boy attempted to penetrate the little girl. As he could not
manage it, they took off his trousers and, to excite him,
Mony gently slapped his backside while Natasha titillated
his miniature gland and tiny balls with the tip of her
tongue. The little boy's cock started to stiffen and he was
thus able to deflower the little girl. When they had been
struggling together for ten minutes, the two were sepa-

rated and Cornabœux seized the little boy and tore his fundament by means of his powerful broad-sword. Mony could not contain his desire to fuck the little girl. He grabbed hold of her, set her astride his thighs and forced his vital organ into her minuscule vagina. The two children let out the most frightful yells and blood streamed round Mony and Cornabœux's cocks.

Next, the little girl was laid on top of Natasha and the priest, who had just finished mass, lifted her skirts and began to beat her charming little white arse. Then Natasha stood up and, straddling André Bar, who was sitting in an armchair, she impaled herself on the conspirator's huge prick. They started a vigorous 'Saint George', as the English say.

The little boy, kneeling in front of Cornabœux, pumped his organ for him with tears streaming down his cheeks. Mony buggered the little girl, who struggled like a rabbit about to have its throat cut. The other conspirators buggered each other, making frightful grimaces. Next, Natasha stood up and, turning round, proffered her arse to all the plotters, who came up one by one and kissed it. At this moment, a wet-nurse with the face of a madonna was led in, her enormous teats swollen with abundant milk. She was made to get down on all fours and the priest began to milk her into the sacred vessels, as if she were a cow. Mony buggered the nurse, whose arse was of a translucent whiteness and stretched to cracking point. To top up the chalices, the little girl was made to piss into them. The conspirators then took communion with a mixture of milk and pee.

Seizing hold of the leg-bones, they swore death to Alexander Obrenović and his wife, Draga Mašin.

The soirée came to an end in an infamous fashion. Some old women were brought in, the youngest of them seventy-four years old, and the conspirators fucked them in every conceivable manner. Mony and Cornabœux left in disgust at about three in the morning. On returning home, the prince stripped to the skin and held out his handsome arse to the cruel Cornabœux, who buggered him eight times on end without withdrawing. They called these daily sessions their little piercing joys.

For some time, Mony carried on with this monotonous life in Bucharest. The King of Serbia and his wife were assassinated in Belgrade. Their murder belongs to history and has already been judged and analysed in various ways. The war between Russia and Japan broke out immediately afterwards.

One morning, Prince Mony Vibescu, stark naked and as handsome as the Apollo Belvedere, was engaged in 69 with Cornabœux. Both were sucking greedily on their respective barley-sugar sticks and weighing with sensual delectation cylinders which had nothing to do with those on phonographs. They ejaculated simultaneously and the prince had his mouth full of spunk when an English valet de chambre, very formal and correct, entered with a letter on a silver-gilt tray.

The letter announced that Prince Vibescu had been appointed, as a foreigner, to the rank of lieutenant, to join General Kuropatkin's army in Russia.

Mony and Cornabœux expressed their enthusiasm for the project by mutual buggerings. They kitted themselves out at once and went to St Petersburg before joining their regiment.

'The war's all right by me,' declared Cornabœux, 'the arses of the Japanese must be appetizing.'

'And the cunts of the Japanese women are certainly delectable,' added the prince, twirling his moustache.

Chapter 5

'His Excellency General Kokodryoff is not receiving visitors at the moment,' said the concierge. 'He is busy putting all his eggs into one little basket.'

'But I am his aide-de-camp,' replied Mony. 'You Petropolitans are ridiculous, with your everlasting suspicions. . . . Can't you see my uniform? I have been summoned to St Petersburg, and not, I imagine, in order to be subjected to the insolence of a mere porter!'

'Show me your papers!' said this Cerberus, a colossal Tartar.

'Here!' said the prince curtly, thrusting his revolver under the nose of the terrified door-keeper, who promptly stood aside to let the officer pass.

With spurs ringing, Mony climbed swiftly to the first floor of the palace belonging to General Prince Kokodryoff, with whom he was to leave for the Far East. There was not a soul about, and this reception astonished Mony, for he had seen his general only the night before, at the Tsar's, and an appointment had been fixed for this very hour.

Mony opened a door giving onto a large, darkened and deserted drawing-room, which he crossed, murmuring to himself:

'Odd, by Jove, but the die is cast, I will play the game to the end. Let us continue our explorations. . . .'

He opened another door which closed automatically behind him. He found himself in a room even darker than the first.

A soft female voice said in French:

'Is that you, Fédor?'

'Yes, it's me, my love!' replied Mony in a low but resolute voice. His heart was pounding like a steam-hammer.

He advanced rapidly towards the sound of the voice and came across a bed. There was a woman lying on it, fully-clothed. She embraced Mony passionately, darting her tongue into his mouth. He responded to her caresses. He lifted up her skirts. She parted her thighs. Her legs were bare and a delicious perfume of verbena emanated from her satiny skin, mingled with the effluvia of the *odor di femina*. Mony placed his hand on her fanny: it was moist. She murmured:

'Let's fuck. . . . I can't wait. . . . Naughty man, you haven't been to see me for a week!'

But instead of replying, Mony, who had pulled out his formidable weapon, climbed thus fully-armed on to the bed, trained his sights and thrust his gun ferociously into the hairy breach of the unknown woman, who immediately began to wriggle her buttocks, saying:

'Put it all the way in. . . . You're making me come. . . .'

At the same time, she put her hand at the root of the organ that was pleasuring her and began to stroke the two little nuts which serve as appendages and are known as testicles, not, as is commonly supposed, because they testify to the consummation of the act of love, but rather because they are the little testae containing the seeds, the grey matter which spurts out of the testis or lower intelligence, just as the head contains the grey matter of the brain, which is the seat of mental functions.

The hand of the unknown woman delicately massaged Mony's balls. All of a sudden, she let out a cry and, with a jerk of her arse, dislodged her ravisher.

'Monsieur!' she cried, 'you have deceived me. My lover has three!'

She leapt off the bed, touched an electric switch and the light came on.

The room was simply furnished: a bed, some chairs,

a table, a dressing-table, a stove. There were several photographs on the table and one represented an officer with a brutal look about him, dressed in the uniform of the Preobrajenski regiment.

The unknown woman was tall. Her beautiful chestnut hair was slightly dishevelled. Her open bodice revealed a full bosom; her two white breasts, veined with blue, nestled cosily in a nest of lace. Her petticoats were chastely lowered. Her face expressing a mixture of rage and stupefaction, she stood her ground before Mony, who was sitting on the bed, cock in air and hands crossed on the hilt of his sword.

'Monsieur,' said the young woman, 'your insolence is worthy of the country you serve. No Frenchman would have been such a cad as to take advantage of this unexpected situation, as you did. I order you to leave this room.'

'Madame or Mademoiselle,' replied Mony, 'I am a Roumanian prince, a newly-appointed officer on Prince Kokodryoff's staff. Having recently arrived in St Petersburg, I am ignorant of the customs of this city, and, although I had an appointment with my superior, I found I could only gain entry to this house by threatening the porter with a revolver. I would have considered it utterly churlish not to satisfy a woman who seemed to be desirous of feeling a member in her vagina.'

'You might at least have told me,' said the unknown girl, looking at his prick, which was beating time, 'that you were not Fédor. And now, go away.'

'Alas!' cried Mony, 'how can it be that you, a Parisienne, are such a prude? . . . Ah! Where will I find women like Alexine Mangetout and Culculine d'Ancône again?'

'Culculine d'Ancône!' exclaimed the young woman. 'You know Culculine? I am her sister, Hélène Verdier; Verdier is her real name, too. I am governess to the general's daughter. I have a lover, Fédor. He is an officer. He has three balls.'

At that moment, they heard a great hullabaloo in the street. Hélène went to look out of the window. Mony looked over her shoulder. The Preobrajenski regiment was marching past. The band played an old air, to which the soldiers were mournfully singing:

> Alas, you poor peasants, you're off to the war,
> They'll fuck your old mothers behind and before,
> The bulls in your stables will service your wives
> And give them the time of their natural lives.
> As for you, all you'll have is Siberian flies
> To tickle your bollocks and give you a rise,
> But on Fridays don't give them a bite of your prick,
> For meat is forbidden, it might make them sick.
> And don't give them sugar or white ration bread,
> They make it by grinding the bones of the dead.
> So come on and fuck now, you young farmer-boys,
> The officer's mare, for she's full of sweet joys,
> And they say that her hole isn't nearly as wide
> As the cunt of a hefty young Tar-ar-tar bride.
> Oh, who cares if they screw all our sweethearts and wives?
> We're off to the wars and we're risking our lives!

Suddenly the music stopped. Hélène cried out. An officer turned his head. Mony, having just seen his photograph, recognized Fédor, who raised his sword in salute and shouted:

'Adieu, Hélène, I'm going to the front. . . . We shall never see each other again.'

Hélène turned as pale as a corpse and swooned away into Mony's arms. He carried her over to the bed.

First, he removed her corsets and her bosom stood up stiffly. She had two superb breasts with rosy points. He sucked them for a moment, then unfastened her skirt, which he took off together with her petticoats and bodice.

Hélène was left in nothing but her chemise. Very excited, Mony lifted the white material that hid the incomparable treasure of two perfectly-formed legs. The stockings came up to the middle of her thighs, which were as round as ivory towers. At the base of her abdomen, the mysterious grotto was concealed in a sacred wood as tawny as autumn leaves. This bush was thick, and between the closed lips of her cunt he could only catch a glimpse of a little slit like the mnemonic notches the Incas used as calendars.

Mony did not take advantage of Hélène's unconsciousness. He pulled off her stockings and began to play 'this little piggie'. Her feet were pretty, as chubby as a baby's. The prince's tongue commenced with the toes of the right foot. Conscientiously, he cleaned the nail of the big toe, then worked his tongue between the digits. He spent a long time on the little toe, which was exceedingly sweet. He noticed that the right foot had a taste of raspberries about it. His licking tongue then poked into the folds of the left foot, upon which Mony discovered a savour that reminded him of Mainz ham.

At this moment, Hélène stirred and opened her eyes. Mony stopped his salty game and looked at the tall, plump beauty stretching herself in pandiculation. Her mouth opened in a yawn, showing a pink tongue between small ivory teeth. Then she smiled.

Hélène: Prince, what have you done to me? Look at the state I am in!

Mony: Hélène! It was for your own good that I made you more comfortable. I have been a Good Samaritan to you. A good deed is never lost, and I have found my exquisite reward in the contemplation of your charms. You are ravishing, and Fédor is a lucky devil.

Hélène: Alas, I shall never see him again! The Japanese will kill him.

Mony: I would be most happy to replace him, but unfortunately I do not have three balls.

Hélène: Don't say that, Mony, it's true you don't have three, but what you have is just as good as his.

Mony: Is that so, my little piglet? Wait while I unbuckle my sword-belt. . . . Ah, that's better. Show me your arse . . . how fat, round and chubby it is . . . just like an angel's cheeks in the act of blowing. . . . Hell's bells! I must give you a spanking in honour of your sister Culculine . . . tap, slap, wham, bam. . . .

Hélène: Ow! Ow! Ow! You're making me hot, I'm all wet.

Mony: What a thick bush you've got . . . slap, wham! I absolutely *must* make your big posterior cheeks blush. You know, he doesn't look angry, this face, in fact when you wriggle he looks as though he's laughing.

Hélène: Come here and let me unbutton you, show me this big baby who wants to warm himself at his mamma's breast. How sweet he is! He has a little red head and he's quite bald. Now here, at the base, at the root, he has hairs and they're hard and black. What a handsome little orphan . . . put him into me, come on! I want to suckle him, Mony, to cuddle and squeeze him and make him come. . . .

Mony: Just a moment while I make you a little rose-leaf. . . .

Hélène: Ah! That's lovely, I can feel your tongue in the slit of my arse. . . . It pierces and forages among the folds of my little rosebud. Don't press out the pleats in my poor arsehole too fiercely, will you, Mony? Wait! Let me make you a good round arse. There! You have buried your whole face between my buttocks. . . . Oh, look out! I'm going to fart. . . . Excuse me, I couldn't hold it in. . . . Ah! Your moustache is prickling me and you are slobbering . . . you pig . . . you're slobbering. Give it to me, give me your big prick to suck. . . . I'm thirsty. . . .

Mony: Ooh! How clever your tongue is, Hélène. If you teach writing as well as you sharpen quills, you must be a magnificent teacher. . . . Oh! Your tongue is pecking at the hole in my tassel. . . . Now I feel it at the root of my knob . . . you are cleaning the foreskin with your hot tongue. Ach! Unrivalled fellatrice, you are an incomparable gobbler! Don't suck so hard. Your little mouth is swallowing the whole of my glans. You're hurting me. . . . Ah! Aaaaaaah! You are tickling all my prick. . . . Ah! Ah! Don't crush my balls . . . your teeth are sharp. That's it, take the tip of the knob . . . let your tongue work there. . . . You love to gobble my cock, eh? . . . little sow. . . . Ah! Ah! Ah! . . . I . . . oh . . . ah . . . I'm com . . . um . . . um . . . ing! Pig! . . . She's swallowed the lot! . . . Come on, give it to me . . . give me your big cunt, let me suck you off till I get another erection. . . .

Hélène: Harder. . . . Work your tongue well on my button. . . . Can you feel my clitoris swelling . . . now . . . do the scissors. . . . That's it. . . . Push your thumb right into my cunt and your index finger into my arse. Ah! It's good . . . so good! . . . Listen, can you hear my belly gurgling with pleasure? . . . Yes, put your left hand on my left nipple . . . crush the strawberry. . . . I'm coming. . . . Oh! . . . can you feel my arse thrusting against you . . . my loins jerking? You bastard! It's good . . . come and suck me. Quick, give me your prick to suck, I'll make him good and hard, let's do 69 . . . you on top. . . .

Swine, you're as stiff as a ramrod, it didn't take long . . . pierce me now. . . . Wait, some hairs have got caught. Suck my tits . . . yes, that's it, good! Go in deep . . . there, stay like that, don't move. . . . I'm squeezing you . . . squeezing my buttocks. . . . I'm going to . . . Oh, I'm dying . . . Mony . . . did you give my sister such pleasure? . . . Push hard . . . it's going right in, piercing my soul . . . it's making me come, like dying. . . . I can't hold it any longer . . . Mony, my darling . . . let's come together. Ah! I can't wait, it's all coming . . . . I'm coming. . . .

Mony and Hélène reached their orgasms at the same moment. Then he licked her cunt clean with his tongue and she did the same to his cock.

While he was adjusting his clothes and Hélène was dressing, they heard a woman crying out in pain.

'It's nothing,' said Hélène, 'they are beating Nadja, Wanda's chambermaid. Wanda is my pupil, the general's daughter.'

'I should like to watch this scene,' said Mony.

The half-dressed Hélène led Mony into a dark, unfurnished room; a false interior window with a two-way mirror looked into the young girl's room. Wanda, the general's daughter, was rather a pretty creature of seventeen. She was brandishing a *nagaïka* with all her strength and thrashing a very attractive young blonde, who was crouched on all fours in front of her with her skirts up. This was Nadja. He arse was magnificent, enormous, overblown. It dandled beneath an unbelievably tiny waist. At each blow of the *nagaïka,* she jumped, and her arse seemed to dilate. The terrible lash had left weals in the shape of St Andrew's cross.

'I won't do it again, Mistress,' cried the whipped girl, and her arse, rising up, revealed a gaping cunt shadowed by a forest of tow-coloured hair.

'Now get out!' shouted Wanda, kicking Nadja in the crotch. The chambermaid ran out howling.

Then the general's daughter went and opened a cupboard and out stepped a little girl of thirteen or fourteen years of age. She was slim and dark-haired and had a very vicious look about her.

'That's Ida, daughter of the dragoman at the Austro-Hungarian Embassy,' Hélène whispered into Mony's ear. 'She and Wanda masturbate each other.'

And in fact, the litle girl threw Wanda on to the bed, lifted her skirts and exposed to the light of day a forest of hair – a virgin forest still – from which emerged a clitoris as long as a little finger. Ida began to suck it frantically.

'Suck hard, little Ida,' said Wanda amorously, 'I am very excited, and you must be too. There is nothing so stimulating as whipping a fat arse like Nadja's. Now stop sucking. . . . I'm going to fuck you.'

The little girl lifted her skirts and placed herself near Wanda. The legs of the latter were large, contrasting singularly with Ida's slender, dark and sinewy thighs.

'Isn't it odd,' said Wanda, 'that I have deflowered you with my clitoris, yet I myself am still a virgin.'

The act had already commenced; Wanda clasped her little friend passionately. For a moment, she stroked the little cunt, which was still almost hairless. Ida said:

'Darling Wanda, my little husband, how hairy you are! Fuck me!'

The older girl's clitoris soon entered Ida's furrow and Wanda's fine, sturdy arse began to plough it furiously.

Mony, beside himself with excitement, slipped a hand under Hélène's skirt and began teasing her skilfully. She performed the same service for him, seizing his plump organ and slowly manipulating it with her hand while the two lesbians embraced distractedly. Mony's engine, with the prepuce pulled back, began to smoke. He bent his knees and squeezed Hélène's little button energetically. Suddenly Wanda, dishevelled and scarlet in the face, stood up and moved away from her little friend, who, snatching the candle from the candlestick, finished off the work begun by the general's daughter's well-developed clitoris. Wanda went to the door and called Nadja. The girl reappeared in a state of terror. On orders from her mistress, the pretty blonde chambermaid unlaced her bodice and drew out her fat tits, then she lifted her skirts and proffered her arse. Wanda's erect clitoris quickly penetrated the hole between the satiny buttocks, and she began moving in and out like a man. Ida, whose now naked breasts were flat but quite charming, continued her game with the candle, seating herself between Nadja's legs and skilfully sucking her cunt. At this moment, Mony ejaculated under the pressure of Hélène's fingers and the spunk squirted onto the window pane that separated them from the Sapphic scene. Afraid their presence would be detected, they left the room.

Arm in arm, they came out into a corridor.

'What did the porter mean,' asked Mony, 'when he said that the general was "busy putting all his eggs into one little basket"?'

'See for yourself,' said Hélène, and, through a half-open door that gave on to the general's study, Mony caught sight of his superior officer in the act of buggering a ravishing young boy. His hair fell to his shoulders in chestnut curls. His eyes, blue and angelic, were as innocent as the eyes of the ephebes, who die young because the gods love them. His handsome arse, white and firm, seemed to accept with a certain prudishness the virile male gift the general was bestowing upon him. The latter bore a distinct resemblance to Socrates.

'The general,' said Hélène, 'tutors his own son, who is twelve years old. The porter's metaphor is quite apt, for the general has found this a convenient method by which to nourish and fertilize the spirit of his male offspring. He inculcates into him, via the fundament, a science which seems to me quite sound, and the young prince will be well fitted to cut a worthy figure in the councils of the Empire when he is a little older.'

'Incest,' said Mony, 'works miracles.'

The general seemed to be at the very peak of pleasure;

he was rolling his bloodshot eyes.

'Sergei,' he cried in a half-strangled voice, 'do you feel in the depths of your being the instrument which, not content with having begot you, has also taken on the task of making you into a perfect young man? Remember, Sodom is a civilizing symbol. Homosexuality would have rendered mankind the equal of the gods, and all evils spring from this desire which the opposite sexes pretend to feel for one another. Today, there is only one means of saving our holy and unhappy Russia, and that is through sodomy; men must declare, once and for all, their Socratic love of buggery, while women must go to the rock of Leucas to take lessons in Sapphism.'

And, letting out a gurgle of voluptuous delight, he shot his spunk into his son's delectable arse.

Chapter 6

The siege of Port Arthur had begun. The valiant General Stoessel was trapped inside with his troops, amongst whom were Mony and his batman, Cornabœux.

While the Japanese were trying to storm the city walls, fortified with barbed-wire entanglements, the defenders, their lives threatened at every moment by the cannonade, consoled themselves by assiduously frequenting the *cafés-chantants* and the brothels, which had remained open.

On this particular evening, Mony had dined lavishly in the company of Cornabœux and a group of journalists. They had enjoyed excellent horse-steaks, fish caught in the port itself and pineapple conserve, washed down with capital champagne.

As a matter of fact, dessert had been interrupted by the untimely arrival of a shell; the explosion destroyed part of the restaurant and killed several of the guests. Mony found this adventure vastly stimulating. With perfect sang-froid, he lit his cigar from the tablecloth, which had caught fire. Then he and Cornabœux left for a *café-concert*.

'That confounded General Kokodryoff,' said Mony on the way, 'was a remarkable strategist; he undoubtedly foresaw the siege of Port Arthur and had me posted here as revenge for catching him in the act of incestuously buggering his son. Like Ovid, I am expiating the crime committed by my eyes, but I have no intention of writing either *Tristia* or *Epistles from Pontus*. I prefer to spend whatever time is left to me in pleasure and self-indulgence.'

Several cannon-balls whistled over their heads; one of

these missiles cut a woman in half and they had to step
over her prostrate body in order to reach the door of
Les Délices du Petit Père.

It was the smartest cabaret in Port Arthur. On enter-
ing, they found themselves in a room filled with smoke.
A red-headed German woman of ample proportions was
singing in a strong Berlin accent. Those of the spectators
who understood German applauded her frantically. Next
came four English girls, the Somebody-or-other Sisters,
who danced a jig, or rather, a cross between a jig, a cake-
walk and a *matchiche. Les girls* were extremely pretty.
Lifting a froth of rustling petticoats, they revealed knickers adorned with frills and furbelows, but felicitously
split down the middle to allow the spectators a glimpse
of plump white buttocks framed in batiste, or a tuft of
dark hair standing out against the whiteness of their bel-
lies. When they kicked up their legs, their bushy cunts
gaped open. They sang:

> *My cosy corner girl*

and were clapped even more enthusiastically than the
ridiculous Fräulein who had preceded them.

Some of the Russian officers, perhaps too poor to buy
women, tossed themselves off conscientiously as they gazed
at this spectacle with their eyes out on stalks, for it was
truly a paradisaical scene, in the Mahommedan sense of
the word. From time to time, one of these pricks shot off
a powerful jet of spunk which spattered a neighbour's
uniform, or even, occasionally, his beard.

After *les girls* had concluded their act, the orchestra
struck up a rollicking march and the *pièce de résistance*
began. A Spanish couple appeared on the stage. Their
matador costumes provoked a lively response from the
audience, who thundered a suitable *Bojé tsaria Krany.*

The Spanish girl was a superb creature, conveniently
double-jointed. Jet-black eyes glittered in a pallid, per-

fectly oval face. Her hips were shapely and as she swayed
the sequins on her costume dazzled the eye.

The torero, strong and svelte, also waggled a fine rump,
and its very masculinity held promise of certain undoubted advantages.

First this interesting pair, with their left hands resting
on their rounded hips, threw a couple of kisses into the
room with their right hands. This caused a furore. Then,
they began to dance in the lascivious style of their native
country. The Spanish girl hoisted her skirts and held
them in such a way that her body remained exposed right
up to the navel. Her long legs were sheathed in red silk
stockings reaching three-quarters of the way up her
thighs, where they were attached to her corset by golden
suspenders which, in turn, were knotted to silk cords
holding a black velvet mask over her buttocks in such a
manner as to conceal the arsehole. Her cunt was hidden
beneath a bush of frizzy, bluish-black hair.

The torero, singing all the while, drew out a very long
and very hard cock. The pair danced thus, stomachs thrust
forward, seeming to seek one another and then flee. The
young woman's belly undulated like a sea suddenly become solid, just as the foam of the Mediterranean solid-
ified to form the pure belly of Aphrodite.

All at once, and as if by enchantment, cunt and cock
united, and it looked as if they were simply going to
copulate on stage. But no, nothing of the kind.

With his cock well-embedded, the torero lifted the
woman into the air, while she bent her knees and let herself be carried about with her feet off the ground. Then,
the stage-hands having stretched a wire at a height of
some three yards above the audience, the Spaniard
climbed up on to it and the obscene tight-rope walker
thus paraded his mistress right across the theatre, over the
heads of the congested spectators. Next, he regained the
stage by walking backwards along the tight-rope. The

applause almost brought the roof down; the audience were full of admiration for the Spanish woman and her charms, especially her masked arse, which seemed to be smiling, for it was wreathed in dimples.

Now it was the woman's turn. The torero, still firmly implanted in his companion's cunt, bent his knees and allowed himself to be walked along the tight-rope.

This acrobatic fantasy had excited Mony.

'Come, let's go to the brothel,' he said to Cornabœux.

The most fashionable whorehouse during the siege of Port Arthur was delightfully named *The Joyful Samurai*.

It was kept by two men, two old symbolist poets who had married for love in Paris and then come to the Far East to enjoy their happiness hidden away from the eyes of the world. They carried on the lucrative profession of brothel-keepers and did very well out of it. They wore women's clothing and called each other 'dearie', without, however, renouncing their moustaches or their masculine names.

One of them was called Adolphe Terré. He was the older of the two. The younger man had been quite a celebrity in Paris at one time. Who can forget the pearl-grey cape and the ermine collar worn by Tristan de Vinaigre?

'We want women,' Mony said in French to the Madame, who was none other than Adolphe Terré. The latter began to recite one of his poems:

One evening, as I pursued a nymph through the rustling
woods*
Between Versailles and Fontainebleau
My cock at this bald chance stood suddenly erect
She passed me upright, slim, diabolically idyllic.
Three times I screwed her, then boozed for thirty days,
I had the clap but the gods looked down and smiled.

---

* *Les Forêts bruissantes:* a reference to Retté's (see note on p. 12) best-known work, *La Forêt Bruissante* (1896).

They saved the poet. Out of my arse wistaria grew
And Virgil shat this Versailles couplet on my head. . . .

'All right, that's enough,' said Cornabœux, 'we want
women, for Christ's sake!'

'Here is the Assistant Madame!' said Adolphe respect-
fully.

The Assistant Madame, that is to say the blond Tristan
de Vinaigre, moved gracefully towards them and, darting
his blue eyes at Mony, recited this historic poem in a
lilting voice:

My prick was flushed with gay vermilion
In the springtime of my years
And my balls hung down like heavy fruit
Longing for a basket.
My cock lies nestled in luxuriant fleece
Snugly swaddled in thick curls
From arse to groin and groin to navel (on all sides, in fact!)
And only my frail buttocks are left bare
Clenched and immobile when I must shit
On to the glossy paper and the too-high table
The steaming turds of my poetic thoughts.

'Look here,' said Mony, 'is this a brothel or a public
convenience?'

'Assemble all the ladies in the drawing-room!' cried
Tristan, at the same time handing Cornabœux a towel
and adding: 'One towel between two, Messieurs . . . you
understand . . . in times of siege.'

Adolphe collected the 360 roubles, which was the price
of visiting a prostitute in Port Arthur. The two friends
went into the drawing-room, where an incomparable
spectacle awaited them.

The whores, dressed in peignoirs of crimson, mauve,
gooseberry green or burgundy, were playing bridge and
smoking Virginia cigarettes.

At that moment, there was an appalling crash; a shell fell through the ceiling and landed heavily on the floor, where it embedded itself like a meteor, right in the middle of the circle formed by the bridge-players. By a happy chance, the shell did not explode. All the women fell backwards screaming. Their legs were flung into the air, exposing the ace of spades to the concupiscent eyes of the two soldiers. There was an admirable display of arses of all nationalities, for this model brothel employed prostitutes of every race. The pear-shaped arse of the Friesian girl contrasted with the full round arses of the Parisiennes, the marvellous buttocks of the English, the square posteriors of the Scandinavians and the drooping bottoms of the Catalans. A negress exposed a tormented mass of flesh that resembled a volcanic crater rather than a female rump. As soon as she was on her feet again, she declared that the enemy camp had won a grand slam, for human beings quickly become accustomed to the horrors of war.

'I'll take the negress,' declared Cornabœux, and this Queen of Sheba, preening herself on being chosen, saluted her Solomon with these affable words:

'Is you gwin' ter prick mah hot p'tato, Genr'l, sah?'

Cornabœux embraced her tenderly. But Mony was not satisfied with this cosmopolitan exhibition.

'Where are the Japanese girls?' he asked.

'They cost fifty roubles extra,' exclaimed the Assistant Madame, twirling his bold moustaches. 'They are the enemy, you understand!'

Mony paid up and a score or so of little Madame Butterflies were brought in, wearing their national costume.

The prince chose a charming girl from the group and the Assistant Madame ushered the two couples into a boudoir suitably furnished and fitted out for the purpose of fucking.

The negress was called Cornelia and the Japanese girl

answered to the exquisite name of Kilyemu, that is, flower bud of the Japanese medlar tree, While they undressed they sang, the one in Tripolitanian dialect, the other in Bitchlamar.

Mony and Cornabœux took off their clothes.

Leaving his batman in one corner with the negress, the prince turned all his attention to Kilyemu, whose child-like and yet grave beauty enchanted him.

He embraced her tenderly, and, from time to time throughout this beautiful night of love, they heard the noise of the bombardment. Shells burst with a soft thud. It was as if an Oriental potentate were putting on a fire-work display in honour of some virgin Georgian princess.

Kilyemu was small but very well made, her body was as yellow as a peach, her little pointed breasts as hard as tennis balls. The hairs around her cunt ended in a little peak of coarse black hair, like the tip of an artist's brush when it is wet.

She lay down on her back and, drawing her thighs up to her stomach with the knees bent, she opened her legs as if they were the pages of a book.

This posture, which a European would have found impossible, astonished Mony.

He immediately tasted her charms. His prick sank to the hilt in an elastic cunt which, seeming large at first, soon squeezed tight in the most amazing fashion.

This little girl, who appeared to be barely of nubile age, had a nutcracker. Mony quickly became aware of this as, after the first voluptuous thrusts he discharged into a fiercely contracted vagina that sucked the very last drop of juice from his cock. . . .

'Tell me your story,' said Mony to Kilyemu while, from the corner, they could hear the cynical grunts of Cornabœux and the negress.

Kilyemu sat up.

'I am the daughter of a *samisen* player,' she said, 'that's a kind of guitar which is played in the theatre. My father represented the Chorus, he played sorrowful airs and recited lyrical stories in verse-form from a stage-box. My mother, the beautiful July Peach, played the principal roles in these long plays, which are so dear to Japanese dramaturgy. I remember they played *The Forty-Seven Ronin, Siguenai the Beautiful* and also *Taiko.*

'Our company travelled from town to town, and I grew up amongst all this wonderful natural scenery, which still springs to my mind in moments of amorous abandon.

'I used to climb the *matsous,* the giant conifers; I watched the beautiful naked Samurai bathing in the rivers, their enormous penises meant nothing to me at that time, and I would laugh with the pretty giggling serving-maids who came to dry them.

'Oh! What it is to make love in my country, which is always full of blossom! To love a sturdy wrestler under the pink cherry-trees and walk down the slopes of the hills, arm in arm!

'A cousin of mine, a sailor who was on leave from the Nippon Josen Kaisha Company, took my virginity one day.

'My mother and father were acting *The Great Thief* and the house was full. My cousin took me for a walk. I was thirteen. He had travelled in Europe and he recounted to me the wonders of a universe of which I was ignorant. He took me into a deserted garden full of irises, dark red camellias, yellow lilies, and lotuses as pink and pretty as my tongue. There, he kissed me and asked if I had ever made love. I told him I hadn't. Then he undid my kimono and tickled my breasts, it made me laugh, but I became very serious when he placed a long, thick, hard prick in my hand.

' "What do you want me to do with it?" I asked him.

'Without answering, he made me lie down, stripped me from the waist down and, darting his tongue into my mouth, he pierced my hymen. I had the strength to cry out, and my cry must have made the reeds and the lovely chrysanthemums tremble, but immediately afterwards sensual delight awoke in me.

'Later, an armourer carried me off, he was as handsome as the Daiboux of Kamakoura, and his organ deserves to be spoken of with religious awe – it was like gilded bronze, and it was inexhaustible. Every evening, before we made love, I believed that I was insatiable, but when I had felt the hot semen pouring into my vulva fifteen times, I was so weary that I had to offer him my rump so that he could satisfy himself, or, when I was too tired, I took his cock into my mouth and sucked until he ordered me to stop! He killed himself in obedience to the laws of *Bushido,* and, by accomplishing this act of chivalry, he left me alone and inconsolable.

'An Englishman from Yokohama took me up. He smelled like a corpse, as all Europeans do, and for a long time I could not bear this odour. And I used to beg him to bugger me so that I would not have that bestial face in front of me, with its gingery side-whiskers. However, in the end, I got used to him and, as he was completely under my domination, I would force him to lick my vulva until his tongue seized up with cramp and he could no longer move it.

'In Tokyo, I had a girl-friend whom I loved to distraction, and she came to console me. She was as pretty as the springtime and her breasts always looked as if two bees were poised on the tips. We satisfied one another with a piece of yellow marble carved at each end into the shape of a prick. We were insatiable, and when we were in each other's arms, we went wild with joy, frothing at the mouth, howling, thrashing together furiously like two dogs gnawing the same bone.

'The Englishman went mad one day: he thought he was the Shogun and wanted to bugger the Mikado.

'They took him away and I went to work as a prostitute together with my friend, until the day when I fell in love with a tall, strong, clean-shaven German, who had a huge, inexhaustible cock. He beat me and I kissed him with tears running down my face. At last, when I was black and blue from his blows, he would make me a present of his cock and I came like a woman possessed, squeezing it with all my strength.

'One day we boarded a boat, he took me to Shanghai and sold me to a pimp. Then my beautiful Egon went away, without so much as a backward glance, leaving me in despair amongst the women of the brothel, who laughed at me. They quickly taught me the trade, but when I have plenty of money I shall go away, live the life of an honest woman and search the world until I find my Egon and feel his penis in my vagina once more and die, dreaming of the pink blossom of Japan.'

The little Japanese girl, straight-backed and solemn, went away like a shadow, leaving Mony, with tears in his eyes, to reflect on the fragility of human passions.

Then, hearing a sonorous snoring, he turned his head and saw Cornabœux and the negress sleeping chastely in each other's arms; they were a monstrous-looking pair. Cornelia's fat arse stuck out, reflecting the moonlight that streamed through the open window. Mony drew his sword from its sheath and pricked this hefty joint of meat.

There were shouts and cries from the drawing-room. Mony, Cornabœux and the negress quitted the boudoir. The drawing-room was full of smoke. A number of Russion officers had come in and, vomiting obscenities, had thrown themselves upon the English girls. The latter, disgusted by the drunken and uncouth behaviour of these old sweats were muttering Damn's and Bloody's for all they were worth.

Mony and Cornabœux stood for a moment contemplating the rape of the whores, then, during a scene of bizarre and collective buggery, walked out, leaving the desperate Adolphe Terré and Tristan de Vinaigre trying to restore order. Hampered by their petticoats, the pair were flapping about ineffectually.

At that precise moment General Stoessel came in and everyone, including the negress, had to rectify his position.

The Japanese had just launched their first assault on the besieged town.

Mony was almost tempted to retrace his steps and see what his general would do, but he could hear desperate cries coming from the ramparts.

Some soldiers appeared leading a prisoner. He was a tall young German; they had found him at the outer perimeter of the defences, looting dead bodies. He shouted in German:

'I am not a thief. I like the Russians, and I came through the Japanese lines, braving all the dangers, to offer myself as a fag, a pansy, a bum-boy. You must be short of women, so you won't turn your noses up at me.'

'Death!' cried the soldiers, 'put him to death, he's a spy, a thief, he was looting the bodies of the dead!'

There was no officer in charge of the soldiers. Mony stepped forward and demanded an explanation.

'You are mistaken,' he said to the foreigner, 'we have plenty of women, but your crime must be avenged. Since you seem so set on it, the soldiers who captured you will bugger you, then you will be impaled. Thus, you will die as you have lived, which is, according to the moralists, the most beautiful way to die. Your name?'

'Egon Müller,' declared the man, trembling.

'Ah, then I know all about you,' said Mony drily. 'You came from Yokohama, and you sold your mistress, the Japanese girl Kilyemu, without shame, like a true pimp. You are a fairy, a spy, a pimp and a robber of corpses – the complete scoundrel in fact. Prepare the stake men, and every one of you is to bugger him . . . you don't get a chance like this every day.'

The handsome Egon was stripped naked. The boy was marvellously beautiful and his breasts were rounded, like those of a hermaphrodite. Seeing these charms revealed, the soldiers drew out their concupiscent pricks.

Cornabœux was touched; with tears in his eyes he begged his master to spare Egon, but Mony was inflexible, the only concession he made was to allow his batman to have his cock sucked by the charming ephebe, who, with his arse thrust out, received the effulgent pricks in his dilated anus one by one, while the soldiers, good creatures that they were, sang sacred hymns to celebrate their capture.

By the time he had received the third ejaculation, the spy was in a joyous transport; he jerked his arse about and sucked Cornabœux's cock as if he had thirty years of life ahead of him.

[. . . *]

When all the soldiers had buggered the prisoner, Mony said a few words into Cornabœux's ear. The batman was still in a beatific state from having his organ pumped.

Cornabœux went to the brothel and returned shortly with the young Japanese prostitute, Kilyemu, who was wondering what they wanted with her.

[. . . **]

---

* *The soldiers set up the stake.*

***Egon is placed on the stake, still with a huge erection. Kilyemu is hoisted onto him. Her ecstatic movements only hasten her lover's death. Mony orders the soldiers to salute the dying, then tells Kilyemu: 'I have fulfilled your wish. . . . At this moment, the cherry trees are flowering in Japan, lovers are wandering through the pink snowfall of fluttering petals.' Then he shoots her in the head.*

Chapter 7

As a result of the summary execution of the spy, Egon Müller, and the Japanese whore, Kilyemu, Prince Vibescu became very popular in Port Arthur.

One day, General Stoessel sent for him and handed him an envelope, with these words:

'Prince Vibescu, although you are not Russian, you are nevertheless one of the finest officers we have. . . . We are expecting relief, but General Kuropatkin will have to hurry . . . if he delays any longer we shall be forced to capitulate. . . . These Japanese dogs are lying in wait for us and sooner or later their fanaticism will get the better of our resistance. You must cross the Japanese lines and give this despatch to the Generalissimo.'

A balloon was prepared. Mony and Cornabœux practised handling the aerostat for a week and then, one fine morning, it was inflated.

The two messengers climbed into the basket, pronounced the traditional words: 'Cast off!' and quickly rose into the region of the clouds; the earth soon appeared to them as an insignificant little thing and they could see the theatre of war neatly laid out below them: the two armies, the squadrons on the sea, while a match which they struck to light their cigarettes left a more luminous trail than those of the giant cannon-balls the belligerents were firing off.

A fair breeze pushed the balloon in the direction of the Russian armies and after a few days' flight they landed and were received by a tall young officer who bade them welcome. It was Fédor, the man with three balls, the former lover of Culculine d'Ancône's sister, Hélène Verdier.

91

Jumping out of the balloon basket, Prince Vibescu said to him:

'Lieutenant, you are a good fellow, and your kind reception compensates us for a good deal of fatigue. Allow me to beg your pardon for having cuckolded you in St Petersburg with your mistress, Hélène, who is the French tutor to General Kokodryoff's daughter.'

'You did the right thing,' replied Fédor, 'and, just imagine, I have found her sister here, a superb girl called Culculine who is working as a waitress in a beer-hall which our officers frequent. It is run by women. She left Paris to earn her fortune in the Far East, and she is making a lot of money, for the officers live riotously, in the manner of people who have little time to live, and her friend Alexine Mangetout is here too.'

'What!' cried Mony. 'Culculine and Alexine here! . . . Take me quickly to General Kuropatkin, I must accomplish my mission first. . . . Then you will take me to this beer-hall immediately.'

General Kuropatkin received Mony affably. His headquarters was a rather well-appointed railway carriage.

The Generalissimo read the message, then said:

'We shall do everything in our power to relieve Port Arthur. Meanwhile, Prince Vibescu, I confer upon you the title of Knight of Saint George. . . .'

Half an hour later, the newly-decorated officer found himself in the *brasserie, The Sleeping Cossack,* in the company of Fédor and Cornabœux. Two women hurried over to serve them . . . Culculine and Alexine, looking utterly delightful. They were dressed as Russian soldiers and wore lace aprons over the wide pants tucked into their boots; their prominent breasts and backsides swelled out the uniform most agreeably. A little cap perched sideways on the head completed the titillating aspect of this military attire. They looked like little chorus girls from some operetta.

'Good Heavens, Mony!' cried Culculine. The prince kissed the two women and asked them to tell their story.

'Certainly,' said Culculine, 'but then, you must tell us everything that has happened to you. After that fatal night, when the burglars left us half-dead beside the corpse of the one whose prick I had bitten off in a moment of insane joy, I knew nothing more until I came to, surrounded by doctors. They had removed a knife which had been planted between my buttocks. Alexine's family took care of her at home, and we heard no news of you. But, when we were able to go out again, we learned that you had returned to Roumania. The affair caused a terrific scandal, my explorer left me when he returned to Paris and Alexine's senator refused to keep her any more.

'Our star began to wane in Paris. War broke out between Russia and Japan. One of my friends had a lover who was organizing a contingent of women to serve in the *brasserie*-brothels which were following the Russian armies, so we signed on, and here we are.'

Then Mony related all that had happened to him, omitting the events that had taken place on the Orient Express. He introduced Cornabœux to the two women but did not tell them that he was the very same burglar who had planted his dagger in Culculine's buttocks.

All these tales led to a vast consumption of alcohol. The hall had filled up with officers in uniform caps who sang to make the rafters ring as they fondled the serving wenches.

'Let's go,' said Mony.

Culculine and Alexine followed them and the five military figures left the entrenchments and made for Fédor's tent.

Darkness had fallen and the sky was spangled with stars. As they were passing the Generalissimo's wagon, Mony was seized with a sudden whim: he made Alexine take off her trousers, which seemed too tight for her arse, and, while the others walked on, stroked this superb backside, which looked like a pale face beneath the pale moon, then, pulling out his fearsome cock, he rubbed it for a moment up and down the crack of her arse, poking it now and then into her arsehole. Suddenly, on hearing the sharp sound of a bugle, accompanied by the rolling of drums, he made a decisive move and his cock descended between the cool buttocks and entered a valley which ended at the cunt. The young man's hands moved round to the front, groped in the bush and began to excite the clitoris. He moved to and fro, his ploughshare working Alexine's furrow, while the girl rocked her lunar arse back and forth gleefully and the moon above seemed to look down and smile in admiration. Suddenly, the monotonous call of the sentries was heard; their cries echoed repeatedly through the darkness. Alexine and Mony took their pleasure in silence and as they came, almost at the same instant and sighing deeply, a shell rent the air and came down, killing several soldiers who were sleeping in a ditch. They died crying out mournfully like children calling their mothers. Mony and Alexine quickly adjusted their clothing and ran to Fédor's tent.

There they discovered Cornabœux, with his flies unbuttoned, kneeling in front of Culculine who had let her trousers down and was showing him her arse. He said:

'No, there's not a mark, one would never guess you had received a knife-wound there.'

Then, standing up, he buggered her, shouting the Russian phrases he had picked up.

Fédor then placed himself in front of her and inserted his weapon into her cunt. For a moment Culculine looked like a pretty youth who was being buggered while he dipped his wick into a woman, for she was dressed as a man and Fédor's prick seemed to be part of her body. However, her buttocks were too plump for this notion to

prevail, and, in any case, her slender waist and the billow-
ing of her breast belied the idea that she was a nancy-boy.
The trio moved together rhythmically and Alexine
approached to tickle Fédor's three balls.

At that moment a soldier outside the tent called loudly
for Prince Vibescu.

Mony went out. The soldier had come as a courier on
behalf of General Munin, to whose presence Mony was
instantly summoned. He followed the courier and, cross-
ing the encampment, arrived at a wagon; as Mony
climbed in, the soldier announced:

'Prince Vibescu.'

The interior of the wagon resembled a boudoir, but
an Oriental boudoir. Luxury and extravagance had run
riot there, and General Munin, a fifty-year-old giant,
received Mony with great courtesy.

He pointed out a pretty woman lying nonchalantly on
a sofa; she was his wife, a Circassian girl of about twenty.

'Prince Vibescu,' said the general, 'having heard of your
exploit today, my wife was determined to congratulate
you personally. Moreover, she is three months pregnant
and, in the way of pregnant women, she has an irresistible
whim – she wants to sleep with you. There she is! Do
your duty. I shall satisfy myself in my own way.'

Without answering, Mony took off his clothes and
began to undress the beautiful Haïdyn who seemed to be
in an extraordinary state of excitement. She bit Mony
while he was undressing her. She was admirably built
and her pregnancy was not yet apparent. Her breasts,
moulded by the Graces, arose as round as cannon-balls.

Her body was supple, plump and streamlined. There
was such an exquisite disproportion between the fatness
of her backside and the slenderness of her waist that Mony
felt his member stand up like a Norwegian pine.

She seized hold of it while he stroked her thighs, which
were plump at the top and tapered down towards the

knees.

When she was naked, he mounted and penetrated her, whinnying like a stallion while she closed her eyes in a state of infinite rapture.

Meanwhile, General Munin had had a small Chinese boy brought in, a sweet little creature who was terrified out of his wits.

His slit eyes blinked in the direction of the copulating couple.

The general stripped him and sucked his little winkie, which was scarcely bigger than a jujube.

Then he turned him round and slapped his skinny yellow bum. Seizing his heavy sabre, he laid it down beside him. Then he buggered the little boy, who appeared to be familiar with this mode of civilizing Manchuria, for he wriggled his small, celestial bum-boy's body with practised skill.

The general said:

'Enjoy yourself, my dear Haïdyn, I am going to enjoy myself too.'

[. . . *]

The Circassian woman was sitting astride Mony, riding him furiously. Her tits bounced and her arse heaved frantically. Mony's hands fondled her marvellously plump buttocks.

[. . .]

The general put the head down and, seizing his wife by the hips, pierced her arse with his organ. This increased Mony's pleasure. The two pricks, separated only by a thin membrane, collided nose to nose, augmenting

---

* *The general penetrates the Chinese boy, and on reaching his climax, decapitates him.*

the pleasure of the young woman, who writhed like a viper and bit Mony. The triple ejaculation took place at the same moment. The trio separated and the general, immediately standing up, brandished his sabre, crying:

'And now, Prince Vibescu, you must die, you have seen too much!'

But Mony had no difficulty in disarming him.

Then he bound him hand and foot and laid him down in a corner of the wagon, near the corpse of the little Chinese. He returned to the general's wife and continued his delectable fornication until morning. When he left her, she was sleeping, tired out. The general was also asleep and still tied up.

Mony went to Fédor's tent; there too they had been fucking all night. Alexine, Culculine, Fédor and Cornabœux were sleeping naked, stretched out pell-mell on top of the covers. The women's cunt-hairs were glued together with spunk and the men's cocks hung down lamentably.

Mony left them sleeping and began wandering through the camp. There was news of an imminent battle with the Japanese. The soldiers were checking their equipment or eating breakfast. The cavalrymen were grooming their horses.

A Cossack whose hands were cold was warming them in his mare's cunt. The beast was neighing softly. Suddenly, the randy Cossack leapt on to a chair behind his animal and, pulling out a prick as long as a wooden lance, slipped it joyfully into the creature's vagina, which must have dripped a very aphrodisiac hippomaniac juice, for the human brute discharged three times, his arse convulsing violently, before he finally withdrew.

An officer who had observed this act of bestiality approached the soldier with Mony. He reproached him sternly for having succumbed to his passion.

'My friend,' he said to him, 'masturbation is a military

virtue. Every good soldier should know that, in wartime, onanism is the only act of love permitted. Toss yourself off, but don't touch women or animals.

'Besides, masturbation is an admirable thing, for it allows men and women to become accustomed to their imminent and prolonged separation. The habits, ideas, clothing and tastes of the two sexes are becoming more and more disparate. It is high time we took account of this fact, and it seems to me essential, if one wishes to be a master in this world, to obey this natural law which will shortly impose itself upon us.'

The officer went away, leaving a pensive Mony to regain Fédor's tent.

Suddenly the prince heard a weird noise, it sounded like Irish keeners wailing over the corpse of some unknown.

As he approached, the sound became clearer, it was punctuated by sharp slaps, as if an insane conductor were rapping his baton on the rail of the rostrum while a muted orchestra played.

Running swiftly, Mony came upon an extraordinary spectacle. A troop of soldiers, under orders from an officer and armed with long, flexible canes, were taking it in turns to lash the backs of condemned prisoners, who were stripped to the waist.

Mony, being of superior rank to the man in charge of the whipping, took command.

Another convicted man was brought along. He was a handsome Tartar lad who spoke almost no Russian. The prince ordered the soldiers to strip him naked before they thrashed him, so that the cold morning air stung his flesh as well as the canes.

He remained impassive, and this irritated Mony; he spoke a few words into the officer's ear. The latter went off and soon returned with a serving-wench from the *brasserie*. She was a buxom waitress and her rump and breasts swelled indecently beneath the uniform she was wearing. This fine figure of a girl, hampered by her tight costume, arrived waddling like a duck.

'My dear girl, you are indecent,' said Mony. 'A woman of your build should not dress like a man. One hundred lashes of the whip will teach you a lesson.'

The unfortunate girl trembled in every limb, but, at a gesture from the relentless Mony, the soldiers stripped her.

Her nudity contrasted singularly with that of the Tartar boy. He was very tall, with an emaciated face and small, malignant eyes that showed no fear; his limbs had that thinness ascribed to John the Baptist after he had been living on grasshoppers for some time. His arms, his chest and his heron-like legs were hairy, his circumcised penis was hardening and swelling as a result of the thrashing he had received, and the knob was purple, the colour of a drunkard's vomit.

The waitress, a handsome specimen of German womanhood from Brunswick, was heavy in the rump; she looked like a sturdy Luxembourg mare let loose among the stallions. Her flaxen hair added a somewhat poetic quality to her looks, and undoubtedly the water-nymphs of the Rhine look very much like her.

Her pubic hair, very light blonde in colour, hung down to the middle of her thighs. This bush covered a prominent mound of Venus. The woman exuded good health and vigour and all the soldiers felt their members stand to attention of their own accord.

Mony asked for a knout and one was brought to him. He handed it to the Tartar.

'And now, you filthy swine,' he shouted at him, 'if you want to save your own hide, don't spare this whore's.'

Without answering, the Tartar examined the instrument of torture with an expert eye; it was composed of leather thongs with iron filings glued to them.

The woman wept and begged for mercy in German. Her pink and white flesh trembled. Mony made her kneel down, then, with a kick, forced her to raise her fat arse. First, the Tartar shook the knout in the air, then, raising his arm energetically, he was about to strike when the waitress, who was quivering in every limb, let out a sonorous fart which made all the spectators laugh, including the Tartar himself. He let the knout fall. Mony lashed his face with a cane, saying:

'Idiot, I told you to thrash her, not to laugh.'

He handed the Tartar the cane and told him to beat the German girl with this first, to get her used to the thrashing. The man began to strike at a regular pace. His organ, immediately behind the victim's fat arse, was erect but, despite his lust, his arm rose and fell rhythmically; the cane was very flexible, whistling through the air then falling smartly on the taut and swollen flesh.

The Tartar was an artist and the blows he struck formed a calligraphic design: at the base of her back, above the buttocks, the word *whore* soon appeared distinctly.

He was loudly applauded while the cries of the German girl became more and more raucous. At each blow of the switch, her arse writhed for a moment, then rose up again, her buttocks squeezed tight then immediately relaxed again, at which moment her arsehole could be seen, and the cunt below it, wet and gaping.

Little by little, she seemed to adjust to the blows. At each whack of the switch, her back rose gently, her arse opened and her cunt relaxed softly as if she had just experienced some unexpected delight.

Presently, she fell forward, as if overcome with pleasure, and at this moment Mony arrested the Tartar's hand.

He handed him the knout again and the man, wildly excited, crazed with lust, began to strike the German woman's back with this cruel weapon. Each blow left several deep and bloody weals for, instead of lifting the knout after each stroke, the Tartar drew it towards him in such a way that the iron filings on the lashes tore off shreds of skin and flesh, which fell on all sides, spattering the uniforms of the randy soldiery with droplets of blood.

The German woman no longer felt the pain, she writhed, she wriggled and gurgled with pleasure. Her face was red, she was drooling, and when Mony ordered the Tartar to stop, all trace of the word whore had disappeared, for her back was now nothing but a bleeding sore.

The Tartar remained on his feet, the bloody knout in his hand; he seemed to be asking for approval, but Mony looked at him contemptuously:

'You began well, but you have finished badly. Your work is deplorable. You thrashed her like an ignorant fool. Soldiers, take this woman away and bring one of her companions to me in this tent here, which is empty. I will deal with this wretched Tartar.'

He sent the soldiers away, some of them carrying the German girl between them, and took the condemned man into the tent.

He began to beat him with all his strength, using two canes. The Tartar, excited by the spectacle he had just witnessed, and in which he had been a protagonist, could not for long restrain the sperm boiling in his testicles. His member stood erect beneath Mony's blows, and the spurting spunk bespattered the canvas walls of the tent.

At this point, another woman was brought in. She was in her chemise for they had surprised her in bed. Her face expressed stupefaction and profound terror. She was a deaf-mute, and harsh, inarticulate grunts escaped from her throat.

She was a good-looking girl, a native of Sweden. Daughter of the owner of the *brasserie,* she had married a Dane, her father's partner. She had given birth four months ago and was breast-feeding the child herself. She was about twenty-four years old. Her breasts swelling with milk – for she was a good wet-nurse – bulged out under her chemise.

As soon as Mony saw her, he sent away the soldiers who had brought her and lifted up her chemise. The Swede's plump thighs seemed like the shafts of pillars and they supported a superb edifice; her bush was golden and slightly frizzled. Mony ordered the Tartar to beat her while he sucked her cunt. Blows rained on the arms of the beautiful mute, but the prince's mouth, lower down, culled the amorous liquor distilled by this boreal cunt.

Then, after removing the woman's chemise, he lay down naked on the bed. She was hot and randy. She climbed on top of him and his prick sank in deep between thighs of blinding whiteness. Her massive backside rose and fell in cadence. The prince took one breast into his mouth and began to suck the delicious-tasting milk.

The Tartar did not remain inactive for a moment, but, making the cane whistle through the air, he rained blows on the two firm globes of the mute's arse, rousing her to intense pleasure. He thrashed her like a madman, striping her sublime arse, marking without mercy the beautiful plump white shoulders and leaving furrows on her back. Mony, who had already expended a good deal of energy, took a long time to reach his climax and the dumb woman, stimulated by the cane, came fifteen times before he reached first post. Then Mony stood up and, seeing the Tartar in a splendid state of erection, ordered him to pierce the handsome wet-nurse from the rear; she still did not seem to be sated. Mony himself picked up the knout and covered the soldier's back with blood, making him yell horribly as he took his pleasure.

The Tartar did not for a moment abandon his post. Stoically bearing the blows of the terrible knout, he attacked the amorous redoubt wherein he was lodged without a pause, and five times deposited his fiery offering in its keep. Then he lay motionless on top of the woman, who was still shaken by voluptuous convulsions.

Now the prince inflicted wounds on him, for he had lit a cigarette and was burning the Tartar's shoulders. Then he put a lighted match under his balls and the scorching pain revived the indefatigable weapon. The Tartar was working up to another orgasm. Mony seized the knout again and struck with all his might, beating the united bodies of the Tartar and the mute; blood gushed, the blows landed with a sharp smack. Mony swore in French, Roumanian and Russian. The Tartar was experiencing a fearful pleasure, but a look of hatred for Mony passed through his eyes. He knew the language of the deaf and dumb and, passing his hand over his love-partner's face, made signs to her which the latter understood perfectly.

Towards the end of this pleasuring, Mony was struck by a new fantasy: he held the tip of his smouldering cigarette on the tip of the mute's wet nipples. A drop of milk pearled out of the elongated tit, extinguishing the cigarette, but the woman let out a roar of terror as she came.

She made a sign to the Tartar, who immediately withdrew. The pair threw themselves upon Mony and disarmed him. The woman took the cane and the Tartar took the knout. With eyes full of hate, and animated by the hope of vengeance, they began cruelly whipping the officer who had made them suffer. In vain Mony cried out and struggled; the blows spared no part of his body. Nevertheless, the Tartar, fearing that his act of vengeance against an officer would have sinister consequences, soon discarded the knout and, like the woman, contented himself with a simple switch. Mony bounced about under the lashing while the woman concentrated her efforts on striking primarily the prince's belly, balls and prick.

During this time, the mute woman's husband had become aware of her disappearance, for the little girl was crying for her mother's breast. Taking the baby in his arms, the Dane went in search of his wife.

A soldier pointed out the tent where she was, without saying what was going on inside. Mad with jealousy, the Dane rushed forward, lifted the tent-flap and stepped in. It was hardly an everyday sight that greeted him: his wife, naked and streaming with blood, in the company of a naked and blood-stained Tartar, was whipping a young man.

The knout lay on the ground. The Dane put down the child, took hold of the knout and with all his strength lashed out at the woman and the Tartar, who fell to the ground howling with pain.

[... *]

The mother snatched away the child. The Tartar dressed in haste and made off; but the Dane, his eyes bloodshot, raised the knout. He was about to deliver a mortal blow to Mony's head when he noticed an officer's uniform lying on the ground. His arm fell, for he knew that a Russian officer is sacred, he may violate, loot, murder, but the wretched civilian who dares to raise a hand against him will be hanged instantly.

[... **]

---

* *Mony picks up the child and violates her; realizing too late, the parents rush at him.*

** See p. 105.

The sleepers had awoken and had washed and dressed themselves.

Throughout the day, preparations were made for the battle, which commenced towards evening. Mony, Cornabœux and the two women shut themselves up in Fédor's tent. The latter had gone to fight at the advance posts. Soon, they heard the first volley of cannon-fire and stretcher-bearers arrived carrying the wounded.

The tent was converted into a casualty ward. Cornabœux and the two women were conscripted to help gather up the dying. Mony remained alone with three wounded Russians, who were delirious.

Then a woman from the Red Cross came in, wearing an elegant fawn overcoat and an armband on her right arm.

She was a Polish noblewoman, and extremely pretty. Her voice was as soft as an angel's and when the wounded men heard it they turned their moribund eyes towards her, thinking it was the Madonna they saw.

She gave Mony some curt orders in that gentle voice of hers. He obeyed like a child, astonished at the energy of this pretty girl and at the strange gleam that flashed now and then from her green eyes.

From time to time, her seraphic face hardened and a cloud of unforgivable vices seemed to darken her forehead. Apparently, this woman's innocence was subject to criminal lapses.

Mony watched her closely and soon perceived that her fingers dabbled longer than was strictly necessary in the wounds.

They brought in a man whose injuries were horrible

**Mony seizes his revolver. He then forces the Dane to bugger his daughter. Afterwards, he tenderly assists the parents to revive their child, but warns the Dane that if he mentions what has happened to anyone, Mony's word will always outweigh his, and he will be hanged.

The Dane's gratitude is genuine and profuse. Mony returns to Fédor's tent.

to behold. His face was bloody and his chest torn open.

The nurse bandaged him with voluptuous pleasure. She put her right hand into the gaping hole and seemed to thrill at the touch of the heaving flesh.

Suddenly the ghoul lifted her eyes and saw Mony looking at her with a disdainful smile from the opposite side of the stretcher.

She blushed, but he reassured her:

'Do not worry, you have nothing to fear from me, I understand better than anyone the sensual delight you are feeling. I too have unclean hands. Take your pleasure with these wounded men, but do not refuse my embrace.'

She lowered her eyes without a word. Mony was soon standing behind her. He lifted her skirts and uncovered a marvellous arse whose buttocks were so tightly clamped together that it was as if they had sworn never to part.

[. . .] She bent forward to allow Mony to enjoy the sight of her arse.

He introduced his dart between the satiny lips of her cunt, from behind, and with his right hand caressed her buttocks while the left groped beneath her petticoats for her clitoris. [. . . *]

Mony began slapping her large arse as it dandled and shook while the lips of her cunt rapidly swallowed the cadaver's column and vomited it up again. The prince's prick soon regained its earlier stiffness and, placing himself behind the nurse, who was on the point of coming, he buggered her like a man possessed.

Afterwards, they adjusted their clothing [. . . **]

'Alas!' cried Mony, 'cruel woman, to whom God has given the mission of finishing off the wounded, who are you? Who *are* you?'

---

* *The nurse indulges her particular perversion of torturing the dying Russian prisoners by abusing their mutilated bodies.*

**Another wounded man is brought in to 'endure this hateful caress'. He dies after she has taken her pleasure.*

'I am,' she said, 'the daughter of the revolutionary prince, Jan Morneski. The infamous Gurko sent him to Tobolsk to die. To avenge myself, and to avenge my mother Poland, I kill Russian soldiers. I would like to kill Kuropatkin and I pray for the death of all the Romanoffs.

'My brother, who is also my lover, and who deflowered me during a pogrom in Warsaw for fear my virginity would become a Cossack's booty, feels the same as I do. He led the regiment under his command astray and drowned them all in Lake Baikal. He told me of his plan before he left. It is in this way that we, we Poles, avenge ourselves on the Muscovite tyranny.

'These patriotic rages have worked on my feelings, my most noble passions have given way to those of cruelty. As you see, I am as cruel as Tamerlaine, Attila and Ivan the Terrible. Formerly, I was as pious as a saint, yet today Messalina and Catherine would seem as gentle as lambs compared to me.'

It was not without a shudder that Mony listened to the confessions of this exquisite whore. He felt that, at all costs, he must lick her arse in honour of Poland, and he told her how he had dabbled indirectly in the conspiracy that ended the life of Alexander Obrenović, in Belgrade.

She listened in admiration.

'Ah, how I long to see the day,' she cried, 'when the Tsar is thrown from his palace window!'

Mony, who was a loyal officer, protested against this defenestration and declared his allegiance to legitimate autocracy:

'I admire you,' he said to the Polish noblewoman, 'but if I were the Tsar, I would wipe out the Poles *en bloc*. They are inept drunkards, forever manufacturing bombs and making this earth unfit to live in. Even in Paris, these sadistic jokers, who are constantly in and out of the Court of Assizes as well as the Salpêtrière prison, worry the lives out of peaceable citizens.'

'It is true,' said the Polish woman, 'that my compatriots stop at nothing, but when their fatherland is restored to them, when they are allowed to speak their own language, then Poland will once more become a land of chivalry and honour, of voluptuous delights and pretty women.'

'You're right!' exclaimed Mony, and pushing the Red Cross nurse on to a stretcher, he began to plough her in a leisurely fashion; all the time he was fucking her, he chatted of distant and seductive topics. It was as if they were composing a *Decameron* in the midst of the pestilence around them.

'You delightful woman,' said Mony, 'let us plight our troth with our souls!'

'Yes,' she said, 'after the war we shall marry and our cruel acts will become famous throughout the world.'

'I wish for that, too,' said Mony, 'but let them be legal cruelties.'

'Perhaps you are right,' said the nurse, 'there is nothing so sweet as doing what is permitted.'

There on the stretcher, they passed into a trancelike state, pressing their bodies together, biting one another and enjoying a profound orgasm.

At that moment shouts rang out; the routed Russian army was being overrun by the Japanese troops.

The horrible cries of the wounded were heard, the rattle of artillery fire, the sinister rumbling of ammunition wagons and the crackle of rifles.

The tent-flap was rudely snatched open and a troop of Japanese poured in. Mony and the nurse barely had time to adjust their clothing.

A Japanese officer advanced towards Prince Vibescu.

'You are my prisoner,' he said, but with a revolver shot Mony stretched him out stone dead, then, before the eyes of the stupefied Japanese, he broke his sword over his knee.

Another Japanese officer came forward, the soldiers surrounded Mony, who acknowledged his captivity. When he came out of the tent in the company of the little Nipponese officer, he saw afar off on the plain the lagging fugitives who were painfully trying to catch up with the routed Russian army.

Chapter 8

As a parole prisoner, Mony was free to come and go in the Japanese camp. He searched in vain for Cornabœux. He noticed that, throughout his wanderings, the officer who had taken him prisoner kept him under surveillance. He wanted to befriend him and eventually succeeded. The man was a Shintoist, and something of a voluptuary. To Mony, he sang the praises of the wife he had left behind in Japan:

'She is charming, always laughing,' he said, 'and I adore her as I adore the Trinity of Ame-no-Minakanushi-no-Kami. She is as fecund as Izanagi and Izanami, creators of the earth and of mankind, and she is as beautiful as their daughter, Amaterasu, the Sun Goddess. While awaiting my return, she thinks of me and plucks the thirteen strings of her *koto* made of imperial polonia wood or plays her *sio* with seventeen pipes.'

'And what about you?' asked Mony. 'Have you never felt like fucking since you've been away at the wars?'

'Well,' said the officer, 'when the urge is too strong for me, I toss myself off whilst looking at obscene pictures!' And he showed Mony some little books full of wood engravings of astounding obscenity. One of these books showed women making love with all sorts of animals: cats, birds, tigers, dogs, fish and even octopuses with their tentacles, armed with suckers, hideously entwined around the bodies of hysterical Japanese girls.

'All our officers and men carry books of this type,' said the officer. 'They can do without women as long as they can look at these priapic drawings and masturbate.'

Mony often went to visit the wounded Russians. In the

casualty ward, he rediscovered the Polish Red Cross nurse who had given him lessons in cruelty in Fédor's tent.

Amongst the wounded was a captain who came from Archangel. His wound was not unduly serious and Mony often sat at his bedside and chatted to him.

One day this man, whose name was Katache, held out a letter to Mony and begged him to read it. The letter stated that Katache's wife was betraying him with a fur trader.

'I adore her,' said the captain. 'I love this woman more dearly than I love my own life, and I suffer terribly, knowing she is with another man, but I am happy, frightfully happy.'

'How can you reconcile these two feelings?' asked Mony. 'They are contradictory.'

'They are mingled within me,' said Katache, 'and I cannot even conceive of voluptuous pleasure without pain.'

'Then you are a masochist?' said Mony, his interest aroused.

'If you like!' the officer acquiesced, 'in any case, masochism conforms to the precepts of the Christian religion. Listen, since you seem to be interested in me, I am going to tell you the whole story.'

'I would like to hear it,' said Mony eagerly, 'but first drink this lemonade to lubricate your throat.'

Captain Katache began thus:

'I was born in Archangel in 1874, and from a very early age I experienced a bitter joy every time I was punished. Each misfortune that befell my family developed this faculty for enjoying misery, and sharpened it.

'Undoubtedly this came about because I was excessively tender-hearted. My father was murdered and I remember that – I was fifteen at the time – I had my first orgasm as a result of this tragedy. The shock and the terror of it made me ejaculate. My mother went mad, and when I went to visit her in the asylum, I masturbated as I listened to her vile and obscene ravings, for she thought she had been turned into a privy, Monsieur, and described all the imaginary arses that shat into her. One day she thought the cesspit was full and they had to lock her up. She became violent and howled for the sewermen to come and empty her. I listened to her in a state of anguish. She recognized me.

' "My son," she said, "you no longer love your mother, you use other lavatories. Sit on me and shit in comfort. After all, *what better place to shit than in one's mother's breast?*

' "And don't forget, my son, the cesspit is full. Yesterday a publican with diarrhoea came and shat into me. I am overflowing, I can't hold any more. You absolutely *must* send for the men to empty the cesspit."

'Believe me, Monsieur, I was profoundly disgusted, and grieving too, for I adored my mother, yet I felt an indescribable pleasure on hearing these foul, unspeakable words. Yes, Monsieur, I enjoyed it, and I masturbated.

'I was made to join the army but, thanks to my connections, I was able to remain in the north. I frequently visited the family of a Protestant pastor who had settled in Archangel. He was English, and had a daughter of such wondrous beauty that my descriptions cannot make you see her even half as beautiful as she really is. One day, we were dancing together at a private party and, at the end of the waltz, Florence put her hand between my thighs, as if by accident, and asked:

' "Are you hard?"

'She had noticed that I had a terrific erection, but she smiled and said to me:

' "And I'm all wet too, but not in your honour. I'm hot for Dyre."

'And she went mincing over to Dyre Kissird, a Norwegian commercial traveller. They stood chatting and laughing for a moment, then the music struck up and off they went in each other's arms, gazing amorously into each other's eyes. I suffered martyrdom. Jealousy gnawed my heart. And if Florence had seemed desirable to me before, then she was infinitely more so now that she had told me she did not love me. As I watched her dancing with my rival, I came. I could imagine them lying in each other's arms and had to turn my back so that no one would see my tears.

'And then, driven by the demons of jealousy and concupiscence, I swore that I would make her my wife. She's a strange girl, Florence, she speaks four languages: French, German, Russian and English, but she doesn't know any of them really well; she speaks in a peculiarly savage jargon of her own. I myself speak very good French and I am deeply versed in French literature, especially the poets of the late nineteenth century. For Florence, I wrote these verses, which I called symbolist, and which were simply a reflection of my sorrows:

The anenome flowers in the chill winds of Archangel
While angels salve with tears the chilblains on their wings;
And the sighs of flower-named Florence descend in dizzying rings
To match the cold thermometer's icy spell.

For Florence, pale choirs in ice-named Archangel
Have toneless oft intoned old Rome's antique lament,
While she to thawing walls returned the compliment
With heavy-scented gifts of heady asphodel.

O Florence! Archangel!

Bay-laurel from the south, northern angelica,
Herbs both, both women one by one draw nigh the well
And fill its sombre depths with flowers and *reliqua*,
With angels' cast-off wings and flowers of Archangel.*

---

* The first two stanzas of this poem appear in an early manuscript of Apollinaire's, now in the Bibliothèque Nationale in Paris. In including them

'In peacetime, life in a garrison in north Russia is very leisurely. Hunting and worldly pursuits are part of military life. Hunting held little attraction for me and my worldly ambitions were summed up in these words: to make Florence my own, Florence, the girl I love and who does not love me. It was a hard task. I suffered a thousand deaths, for she despised me more and more, she jeered at me and flirted with the polar-bear hunters and the Scandinavian merchants. On one occasion, when a lamentable French musical comedy troupe had come to our distant backwater to give a show, I even surprised Florence skating hand in hand with the tenor, a repulsive billy-goat from Carcasonne. This happened during an aurora borealis.

'But I was rich, Monsieur, and Florence's father was not indifferent to my suit, so I finally married her.

'We left for France and she would not allow me to kiss her once on the journey. We arrived in Nice in February, during the carnival.

'We rented a villa and one day during the battle of flowers, Florence announced that she had decided to lose her virginity that very evening. I thought my love was about to be rewarded at last, but alas! my erotic Calvary was just beginning.

'Florence added that I was not the man chosen to fulfil this function.

' "You are too ridiculous," she said, "and you wouldn't know how to do it. I want a Frenchman, the French are gallant and expert lovers. I shall choose the man who is

---

in *Les onze mille verges* he is perhaps half indulging his leanings towards Symbolist verse and half mocking them.

The reference in the third stanza to '*baie de laurier*' probably refers to Marie Laurencin, with whom Apollinaire had a long affair. '*Angélique*' in the same line is perhaps a reference to his mother. Angélique was his mother's Christian name and a character of the same name plays a central role in *L'Enchanteur Pourrissant*, which is written in a similar, obscure Symbolist style. (I am grateful to Professor S. J. Lockerbie at Stirling University for the above information.)

to deflower me during the fête."

'Accustomed to obedience, I bowed my head. We went to the battle of flowers. A young man with a Nice or Monaco accent kept looking at Florence. She turned her head and smiled at him. I suffered more than the soul suffers in any of the circles of Dante's Inferno.

'During the battle of flowers, we saw him again. He was alone in a carriage decorated with a profusion of rare flowers. We were in a Victoria which was enough to drive one insane, for Florence had insisted that it be entirely decorated with tuberoses.

'When the young man's carriage passed ours, he threw flowers at Florence; she looked at him amorously and threw bouquets of tuberoses.

'In a sudden fit of pique, she hurled a bouquet at him, very hard, and the soft, viscous flowers left a stain on the fop's clothing. Immediately Florence apologized and, without more ado, stepped down and climbed into the young man's vehicle.

'He was a rich *Niçois*, whose wealth came from the olive oil business left to him by his father.

'Prospéro, for such was his name, welcomed my wife without fuss and at the end of the battle his carriage won first prize and mine second. The band was playing. I saw my wife holding the banner my rival had won and kissing him full on the lips.

'That evening, she insisted on dining with me and Prospéro, whom she brought to our villa. It was a glorious night and I felt wretched.

'My wife made us both come into the bedroom, I grieving to death and Prospéro astonished, and a little embarrassed, at his good fortune.

'She pointed to an armchair and said to me :

' "Sit there and learn a lesson in the voluptuous arts, try to pick up something from it."

'Then she told Prospéro to undress her, which he did

with a certain grace.

'Florence was enchanting. Her firm flesh, plumper than one would have supposed, thrilled under the touch of the young *Niçois*. He undressed too and his prick was erect. I noted with pleasure that it was no bigger than mine. In fact, it was smaller and pointed. In other words, just right for a virgin. They made a delightful pair; she was all rosy in her lace chemise, her hair elegantly dressed, her eyes sparkling with desire.

'Prospéro sucked her breasts, which were pointed like preening doves, and, passing his hand under her chemise, he stroked her a little while she amused herself by pressing his cock down then letting go suddenly so that it slapped back against his belly. I was crying in my arm-chair. Suddenly, Prospéro took my wife in his arms and lifted her chemise at the back; her pretty, chubby bottom appeared, full of dimples.

'She laughed while Prospéro slapped her, making roses mingle with the lilies of her backside, but soon her mood changed and she said gravely:

' "Take me."

'He carried her over to the bed and I heard her cry out in pain as her ravisher's penis tore the hymen in its passage.

'They took no further notice of me. I was sobbing, yet enjoying my agony, and no longer able to contain myself, I pulled out my cock and had a wank in their honour.

'They fucked about ten times. Then my wife, as if suddenly remembering my presence, said to me:

' "Come and see, dear husband, what a good job Prospéro has made of it."

'I approached the bed, my prick wagging, and my wife, seeing that my member was much larger than Prospéro's, conceived a sudden contempt for him. She stroked my cock, saying:

' "Prospéro, your cock is not worth a light, even my

husband, who is a half-wit, has a bigger one than yours. You have cheated me. My husband will avenge me. André" – that's my name – "whip this man till you draw blood."

'I threw myself upon him and, seizing a dog-whip that was lying on the bedside table, I whipped him with all the strength lent to me by jealousy. I whipped him for a long time. I was stronger than he was and finally my wife took pity on him. She made him dress and sent him away, saying goodbye to him forever.

'When he was gone, I thought my sorrows were at an end. Alas! She said to me:

' "André, give me your prick."

'She masturbated me but would not let me touch her. Then she called her dog, a beautiful Great Dane, and rubbed his tool for a moment. When his pointed prick was erect, she made the dog mount her, ordering me to help the beast. His tongue was lolling out and he was panting with lust.

'My suffering was so intense that I fainted as I climaxed. When I came to, Florence was calling me urgently. The dog's penis, once it had penetrated, refused to come out again. For half an hour both the woman and the beast had been making fruitless efforts to separate. A nodule on the Great Dane's prick held it firmly in my wife's clenched vagina. I threw cold water over them and this soon restored them to liberty. Since that day, my wife has shown no desire to make love with dogs. As a reward, she masturbated me, then sent me off to bed in my own room.

'Next evening, I begged my wife to allow me my marital rights.

' "I adore you," I told her, "nobody could love you as I do, I am your slave. Do with me what you will."

'She was naked and utterly ravishing. Her hair was spread out on the pillow, the strawberries on her breasts drew me, and I wept with frustration. She took out my cock and slowly, with short strokes, tossed me off. Then she rang the bell and a pretty chambermaid, whom she had engaged in Nice, came in in her nightdress, for the bell had summoned her from her bed. My wife made me take my place in the armchair again, and I watched the revels of these two tribades who slobbered and panted as they feverishly indulged in their pleasures. They played pussy, rubbing themselves off on each other's thighs, and I saw young Ninette's arse, large and solid, mounting above my wife's face, and Florence's eyes drowning in sensual rapture.

'I wanted to join in with them, but the pair of them laughed at me, they tossed me off then plunged back into their unnatural joys.

'Next day, my wife's choice fell not on Ninette but on an officer of the *Chasseurs Alpins*. It was his turn to torture me. His male organ was enormous and swarthy. He was a coarse fellow, he insulted me and beat me.

'When he had fucked my wife, he ordered me to come close to the bed and, taking up the dog-whip, he lashed me over the face. I cried out in pain. Alas! My wife burst out laughing, rekindling in me that bitter-sweet delight I had already experienced in the past.

'I let this brutal soldier undress me, for he needed to whip me in order to excite himself.

'When I was naked, the officer insulted me, calling me "cuckold" and "horned beast", then lifting the whip, he brought it down on my behind. The first blows were savage. But I saw that my wife was taking a delight in my sufferings, and her pleasure became my own. Yes, I take pleasure in suffering.

'Each blow that fell was like a rather violent sensual pleasure on my buttocks. The first burning pain had soon turned to an exquisite tickling and my prick was rampant. The lash had soon lacerated my skin, and the blood that ran down from my buttocks had rekindled me in a strange way. It considerably heightened my pleasure.

'My wife's finger was dabbling in the froth that clung around her pretty cunt. With her other hand she was tossing off my torturer. The blows suddenly redoubled and I felt the moment of orgasm approaching for me. My brain was in a whirl; the martyrs honoured by the Church must have experienced such moments.

'I got up, bloody and erect, and threw myself on my wife.

'Neither she nor her lover could stop me. I fell into my wife's arms and no sooner had my member touched the hairs of her adored cunt than I came, letting out wild and horrible cries.

'But the Alpine soldier immediately tore me from my position; my wife, scarlet with rage, said I must be punished.

'She picked up some pins and, one after the other, stuck them into my flesh with voluptuous pleasure. I cried out under the appalling pain. Any man would have taken pity on me, but my unworthy wife lay back on the red bed and, spreading her legs wide, pulled her lover towards her by his great ass's prick, then, opening the hair and the lips of her cunt, she thrust his member in, right up to the balls, while her lover bit her breasts and I rolled on the floor like a maniac, driving the painful pins still deeper into my body.

'I woke up in the arms of the lovely Ninette, who was crouched over me pulling out the pins. I could hear my wife in the next room, swearing and crying out with pleasure as she lay in the officer's arms. The agony of the pins Ninette was extracting, together with the pain my wife's pleasure caused me, made my cock swell up fearfully.

'Ninette, as I said, was crouched over me. I seized her by her bush and felt the wet slit beneath my fingers.

'But, alas! at that moment the door opened and a horrible *botcha,* that is to say, a bricklayer's mate from Piedmont, came in.

'The man was Ninette's lover, and he flew into a furious rage. He pulled up his mistress's skirts and began beating her in front of me. Then he took off his leather belt and thrashed her with that. She cried out:

' "But I didn't make love with my master."

' "That's why he was holding you by the hairs of your arse," said the bricklayer.

'Ninette tried in vain to defend herself. Her large arse twitched beneath the blows of the lash, which whistled and cut through the air like a snake making a strike. The cheeks of her arse were soon on fire. She evidently enjoyed this sort of correction, for she rolled over and, seizing her lover's flies, unbuttoned him and drew out a cock and balls that must have weighed at least seven pounds altogether.

'The swine had a hard-on like a ramrod! He lay down on top of Ninette and she crossed her legs over the workman's back. I saw the thick sword enter a velvety cunt which swallowed it like a lozenge and regurgitated it like a piston. Their pleasure ended in a prolonged orgasm and their cries mingled with my wife's.

'When they had finished, the *botcha,* who had red hair, stood up and, seeing that I was rubbing my prick, insulted me, took up the whip again and thrashed me all over. The beating hurt me dreadfully, for I was weak and I no longer had the strength to feel sexual delight. The buckle bit cruelly into my flesh. I cried out: "Mercy!"

'But at that moment my wife came in with her lover and, as there was a barrel-organ playing a waltz beneath our windows, the two depraved couples began to dance on my body, crushing my balls, my nose, and making me bleed from head to foot.

'I fell ill. But I got my revenge, for the *botcha* fell off

some scaffolding and broke his skull, and the Alpine officer, having insulted a comrade, was killed by him in a
duel.

'An order came from His Majesty, calling me to serve
in the Far East, so I have left my wife, who is constantly
deceiving me. . . .'

And that was the end of Katache's tale. It had inflamed
both Mony and the Polish nurse, who had come in towards the end of the story and listened, quivering with
repressed lasciviousness.

The prince and the nurse hurled themselves on the
unfortunate patient, stripped him and, seizing some Russian flagpoles that had been captured in the last battle
and were lying about on the ground, began to beat the
wretched man. His behind jerked at each blow. He cried
out in delirium:

'Oh, my darling Florence, is it your divine hand that
strikes me once more? You're making me hard. . . . Each
blow thrills me. . . . Don't forget to toss me off. Oh!
That's good. You're hitting my shoulders too hard. . . .
Oh! that blow made the blood spurt. . . . It flows for you
. . . my wife . . . my turtle dove . . . my dearest little
fly. . . .'

The whore of a nurse struck him as no one has ever
struck before. The victim's arse heaved, livid and stained
here and there with anaemic-looking blood. Mony's heart
shrank, he became aware of his own cruelty and his fury
turned against the infamous nurse. He lifted her skirts
and began to beat her. She fell to the floor, moving her
vicious haunches, which were enhanced by a beauty spot.

He struck with all his might, making the blood spout
from the satiny flesh.

She rolled over, crying out like a woman possessed.
Then Mony's stick landed on her belly, making a hollow
sound.

He had a brilliant inspiration and, picking up the

other stick, which the Red Cross woman had dropped, he began to play a drumroll on her naked belly. The tum-tum-tum's followed the tara-tara-ta's with dizzying speed, and even little Bara, of glorious memory, did not beat the drum so well at the charge on the Arcole bridge.

Finally the abdomen split open; Mony kept on drumming and, outside the infirmary, the Japanese soldiers, thinking it was the call to arms, assembled. Bugle-calls sounded the alert in the camp. From all directions, the regiments ran to form up, and it was very lucky that they did so, for the Russians were just about to start an offensive and were advancing towards the Japanese camp. If it had not been for Prince Vibescu's drum-call, the Japanese camp would have been captured. Moreover, this was the decisive victory for the Japanese. It was entirely due to a sadistic Roumanian.

Suddenly some male nurses came into the room carrying wounded men. They saw the prince beating the burst abdomen of the Polish noblewoman. They saw the wounded man, lying naked and bleeding on his bed.

They rushed at Mony, bound him and carried him away.

A court martial condemned him to death by flagellation, and nothing would make the Japanese judges relent. An appeal to the Mikado for mercy met with no success.

Prince Vibescu accepted his fate courageously and prepared to die as a true hereditary Hospodar of Roumania.

Chapter 9

The day of the execution arrived. Prince Vibescu confessed, took communion, made his last will and testament and wrote to his parents. Later, a twelve-year-old girl was let into his prison cell. He was amazed at this, but, since they left her alone with him, he started to cuddle her.

She was a charming child, and told him in Roumanian that she came from Bucharest and had been taken prisoner by the Japanese among the rearguard of the Russian army, for her parents were army victuallers.

Her captors had asked her if she would like to sacrifice her virginity to a Roumanian condemned to death, and she had accepted.

Mony lifted her skirts and sucked her little rounded cunt, which was still quite hairless, then he slapped her playfully while she tossed him off. Then he put the knob of his cock between the little Roumanian's childish legs, but he could not enter. She assisted him in his efforts, thrusting her bottom forward and offering her little breasts, as round as mandarins, for the prince to kiss. He went into an erotic frenzy and his prick finally penetrated, ravishing her maidenhead and making the innocent blood flow.

[. . . *]

The Japanese soldiers came in then and marched him out. A herald read the sentence in the courtyard of the prison, which was an ancient Chinese pagoda of marvel-

---

* *Mony kills the child.*

123

lous architecture.

The sentence was brief: the condemned must receive a blow of the scourge from each Japanese soldier camped in this place. The garrison consisted of eleven thousand men.

While the herald read the sentence, the prince recalled to mind his turbulent life. The women of Bucharest, the Serbian Vice-Consul, Paris, the murders in the sleeping-car, the little Japanese whore in Port Arthur – all these came dancing through his memory.

One fact stood out: he remembered the boulevard Malesherbes, Culculine in her spring dress trotting towards the Madeleine, and he himself saying to her:

'If I don't make love to you twenty times in succession, may I be punished by the eleven thousand virgins, or even eleven thousand *verges*.'

He had not fucked her twenty times in succession, and now the day had arrived when he was to be punished by eleven thousand scourges.

He was lost in his reverie when the soldiers shook him and led him before his executioners.

The eleven thousand Japanese were lined up in two rows, facing one another. Each man held a flexible switch. Mony was stripped, then he was forced to march down this cruel avenue bordered with torturers. The first blows did no more than make him jump. They fell on a satiny skin, leaving dark red marks. He bore the first thousand blows stoically, then fell down in a pool of his own blood, with his cock erect.

Then he was put on a barrow and the lugubrious procession continued, accompanied by the sharp, rhythmic blows of the scourges, which beat on swollen and gory flesh. Soon his prick could no longer retain the jet of sperm and, engorged to bursting point, spat out its whitish liquid into the faces of the soldiers, who beat still harder on this tattered shred of humanity.

At the two-thousandth blow, Mony delivered up his soul. The sun was dazzling. The singing of the Manchurian birds made the radiant morning still brighter. The sentence was carried out to the letter, and the last soldiers flayed a kind of shapeless rag, a lump of sausage meat which no longer had any recognizably human characteristics, except for the face, which had been scrupulously respected and wherein the glazed eyes, open wide, seemed to contemplate the divine majesty of the Beyond.

Just then, a convoy of Russian prisoners passed near the place of execution. They were made to stop and watch, as an impressive warning to the Muscovites.

But a cry rang out, followed by two others. Three prisoners darted forward and, as they were not chained, threw themselves upon the body of the executed man, who had just received the eleven-thousandth blow of the scourge. They fell to their knees and, shedding tears, kissed Mony's bloody head with devotion.

The Japanese soldiers, momentarily stunned, soon realized that though one of the prisoners was a man, and a Hercules at that, the other two were pretty women disguised as soldiers. In fact, it was Cornabœux, Culculine and Alexine, who had been taken prisoner after the disastrous defeat of the Russian army.

At first the Japanese respected their grief, then, their lust aroused by the sight of the two women, they began to torment them. Leaving Cornabœux on his knees beside his master's corpse, they stripped the trousers off Culculine and Alexine, who struggled in vain.

The pretty Parisian girls' lovely white arses, thrashing and jerking about, were soon revealed to the admiring gaze of the soldiers. They began to whip these charming posteriors gently and without anger, as they bobbed about like drunken moons, and when the beauties tried to get up, the hairs of their gaping cunts were visible below.

Blows slashed through the air and, falling flat but not

too hard, marked for an instant the solid, fat arses of the Parisian girls, but the marks were quickly effaced, only to re-form at the spot where the switch struck anew.

When they were suitably excited, two Japanese officers led them into a tent and there they fucked them a dozen times with the fury of men who have been starved by very long abstinence.

These Japanese officers were gentlemen of noble families. They had been on espionage work in France and knew Paris. Culculine and Alexine had no difficulty in obtaining their promise to deliver up the body of Prince Vibescu. They pretended that they were sisters and that he was their cousin.

Amongst the prisoners there was a French journalist, who was war correspondent of a provincial paper. Before the war he had been a sculptor, and not without merit; his name was Genmolay. Culculine sought him out and implored him to sculpt a monument worthy of the memory of Prince Vibescu.

Genmolay's great passion was flagellation. All he asked of Culculine was permission to whip her. She accepted and arrived at the appointed hour with Alexine and Cornabœux. The two women and the two men stripped naked. Alexine and Culculine lay down on a bed, their heads down and their arses in the air, and the two stalwart Frenchmen, armed with switches, began to strike in such a way that most of the blows fell in the cracks of their arses or on their cunts which, on account of their posture, were admirably prominent. The beating excited all the participants. The two women suffered martyrdom, but the thought that their sufferings would procure a suitable sepulchre for Mony sustained them right to the end of this singular ordeal.

Then Genmolay and Cornabœux sat down and made the women suck off their thick cocks full of sap, while they continued to beat the girls' trembling posteriors with their switches.

Next day, Genmolay set to work. He had soon completed a most extraordinary monument, surmounted by the equestrian statue of the prince.

On the pedestal were bas-reliefs representing the renowned feats of Mony Vibescu. On one side, he was to be seen leaving the besieged Port Arthur by balloon, and on the other, he was shown as a patron of the arts which he had gone to study in Paris.

The traveller who crosses the Manchurian countryside between Mukden and Dalny suddenly perceives – not far from a battlefield still strewn with bones – a monumental tomb in white marble. The Chinese who till the fields around it revere it, and the Manchurian mother, in reply to her child's questions, tells him:

'It is a giant cavalier who protected Manchuria against the devils of the West and of the East.'

But generally the traveller prefers to ask the level-crossing keeper of the Trans-Manchurian railway. This guard, dressed as an employee of the P.L.M., is a Japanese with slit eyes. He replies modestly:

'It is a Japanese drum-major who played a decisive part in the victory of Mukden.'

But if, in his curiosity to acquire precise information, the traveller approaches the statue, he remains pensive for a long time after he has read this verse engraved on the pedestal:

> Here lie the bones of Prince Vibescu
> Unrivalled lover of the eleven thousand scourges
> Better by far, oh, you who pass this place!
> To have deflowered the eleven thousand virgins.